TALES FROM THE
BACKWARDS Z

Marshall McGaw

authorHOUSE®

AuthorHouse™
1663 Liberty Drive
Bloomington, IN 47403
www.authorhouse.com
Phone: 1-800-839-8640

Published by AuthorHouse   04/24/2012

ISBN: 978-1-4685-5054-2 (sc)
ISBN: 978-1-4685-5053-5 (hc)
ISBN: 978-1-4685-5052-8 (e)

Library of Congress Control Number: 2012902076

Marshall McGaw
marshallmcgaw@cox.net

Dedication

I dedicate this book to my wife Jean who has stuck with me through thick and thin for over three decades. She raised my three children and kept my grandchildren quiet while I put my thoughts down on these pages.

TALES FROM THE BACKWARDS Z

Mount Pleasant is a small town of four thousand or so people nestled in the beautiful rolling hills of southern Middle Tennessee. It is an old southern town with the classic two-story red brick buildings lining Main Street and a statue of a Civil War soldier standing tall and proud in the center of the town square. As I was growing up, I assumed my town was just like the many other small towns scattered around the south.

In the days before the interstate system was fully developed, my family would take trips and pass through many of these small towns that I was sure were just like my town. It was normal to see people sitting in rocking chairs on wood-framed front porches smiling and waving as we drove by. We always waved back, even though we had never seen them before and would probably never see them again. They sure as heck had never seen us before. Each town had a town square that appeared to have been dropped into the middle of the main road causing travelers to navigate around the obstruction before resuming course towards the next town.

It wasn't until I moved away and started telling these hilarious stories about the various characters from the Mount Pleasant area that I realized that although my town looked just like these places I passed through as a child, there was something different about the place where I grew up. People seemed to be intrigued as I passed these stories on and rarely walked away until the end of the story was revealed. It was during these sessions that took place a long way from home that I came to realize that there is probably no other place like my town in the south, or for that matter, east of the Mississippi River. I haven't done enough traveling west of the Mississippi to know for sure, but I seriously doubt a town like mine exists 'out yonder' either.

When a resident of Mount Pleasant first receives a license to operate a car or pickup truck, most will soon afterwards begin to cruise a route called 'The Z'. The Z was given its name by an earlier generation of travelers because of its design. The route begins at Zingarell's Market on the southwest edge of town, proceeds east about a half mile to Washington Avenue, then northwest for a mile or so on Washington until the driver nears the top of Rippey's Hill. An east turn on Fairview Drive carries the traveler on the last half mile of the route. If a photographer took an aerial photograph from ten thousand feet or so and traced this route, it would form a perfect Z . . . well, a backwards Z . . . but The Z is the name passed on from earlier generations that probably never actually thought about the fact it was backwards.

After hanging a right on Haylong Avenue at the end of The Z, the driver eventually works his or her way back west to the original starting point. After taking a long swoop through the two acre, usually half-empty parking lot of Zingarell's Market, the route is repeated . . . and repeated. This is called cruising or driving around in other towns. My town simply has a defined route with several vacant parking lots along the way allowing folks to easily stop and chat with other local travelers of The Z.

I grew up on Fairview Drive which is on the last leg of the Z. As a youngster, I would sit on the porch and watch the teenagers drive by and couldn't wait until my time came. When it finally did, I put several thousand miles on a couple of old pickup trucks cruising the Z and idled away a few hundred gallons of gas at the various stopping and chatting points. It was this time I spent wasting time along the route that I heard tales of the past exploits of some local characters that grew up in and around my town. I also passed on a few stories about some dumb stuff I had been involved in too.

Were some of these exploits embellished as they were passed around through the years from person to person like the school yard game of gossip? All I can tell you is that I was directly involved in many of the stories I am about to tell you. I can raise my right hand and tell you that these are completely true. As for the stories about the other characters from years gone by, I personally know most of these people in the stories and believe these things happened . . . at least close to the way I tell it.

Even if these things didn't happen exactly the way history has been passed down to me, these stories are a heck of a lot of fun to hear about and I have a blast passing them on. So . . . is there another place like Mount Pleasant Tennessee? I will let you decide that.

GROUNDHOG DAY

C ALL US DERANGED, but put eight or nine neighborhood kids together ages ten to fourteen and you will get some weird ideas. We lived on the edge of town on the last leg of The Z and had a lot of trees, thus a lot of wildlife. Seeing a dead bird was a regular occurrence for us as we strolled around the neighborhood. One not so windy day we were attempting to fly our kites we had purchased the day before at Couch's Dime Store. Each kite would go about the height of a telephone pole and then fall back to the ground.

Bobby Hayes had a huge evergreen bush in his front yard. You could crawl under the low hanging branches and eventually work your way into the middle of the bush to what appeared to be a natural hidden fort. Kids like forts. It would hold four kids comfortably but there were times we had half the neighborhood in there.

This particular morning was full of disappointments as kites continuously fell to the ground. We came up with the idea that we could take this kite string that was meaningless to us on windless days, tie it to the foot of a dead bird, and throw the bird over the power line that crossed over the intersection of Washington Avenue and Fairview Drive. We would then patiently wait until a vehicle came by. The unsuspecting vehicle, having to slow down at the intersection, was an easy target. Just as it went under the bird, we would release the string. The bird would drop at thirty two feet per second per second onto the vehicle, preferably in the middle of the windshield for best results. It took us a few days to perfect this, but we got to the point that we could put a dead bird in the center of a windshield a high percentage of the time. It was an art.

As weeks went by, every kid in the neighborhood perfected the placement of a bird on an unsuspecting vehicle. This was before the days of video games. We had heard Atari had a ping pong game you could play on a television set, but nobody in our neighborhood had actually seen one. Doing puzzles was for the kids whose parents wouldn't allow them to hang out in the neighborhood with us.

This was so much fun that I am sure all of us would have done this well into mid-life if it were not for 'groundhog day'. We found a big dead one lying in ole man Hildreth's vacant lot. To most of us it was just a dead groundhog. I had seen dozens of them and was about to walk away in my search of another dead bird to tie my string to. Most cars left hurriedly when our birds hit their windshield, many times taking the bird, so we had to replace our birds regularly. But Hayes was a genius in the art of pranks. He had his string pulled from his pocket (we all carried our own roll of kite string now as if it were a weapon) and tied around the groundhog's foot before any of us knew what was going on. It never occurred to us amateurs to use a groundhog.

Have you ever tried to throw a dead groundhog over an eighteen foot high power line? Next time you come upon a dead one, try it. I am sure a raccoon or an armadillo would also serve as a good example . . . or try a brick.

We took turns attempting to hurl this groundhog over the power line until we were all huffing and puffing. We could get it up to about sixteen feet in the air which was two feet short. We would have to run and hide every time we heard a car coming up Washington Avenue, so this was taking a good part of our day.

Hayes eventually went into his garage and came out with his dad's five foot step ladder. Now try this: balance yourself on the top rung of a step ladder, swing a dead groundhog around your head as if you were about to rope a calf, and attempt to throw it over a power line. Remember that every time you hear a car coming you have to grab the groundhog, wad up the string, fold the ladder up, and run and hide in the bushes. Where were our parents? We had windows in our houses. Where were the police?

I don't remember which one of us finally got it over the power line. I don't know why I don't remember because this should have gone down in neighborhood history, but all I remember is that it wasn't me. I did attempt it at least twenty times. By the time we had the groundhog in place the sun had set in the west and it was dark outside. The large, round groundhog looked to be the size of the moon hanging upside down over the corner of Fairview and Washington with the star lit sky as a back drop. We had to work the string back and forth to get it over the downhill lane. We had figured out by trial and error using birds through the weeks that this was the best lane to make the drop.

I was in the bush with Hayes, my sister Leslie, and a couple of the younger kids that were following us as we set a good example for them. We were going to drop this groundhog on the next vehicle that came by. It could have been a Cadillac or a Volkswagen, an old driver or a teenager . . . it didn't matter. Maybe it was fate if there is such a thing, but the next vehicle to come down the road was a Jeep Wrangler with the top pulled down. Did I mention it was summertime?

This Wrangler was packed with teenage girls and it was my turn to drop. I could put a Blue Jay on the center of a windshield of a car doing twenty-five miles per hour, but I had never dropped a groundhog before. None of us had. Probably nobody in the world had. Probably nobody in the world has since. What kind of moron would do that anyway?

My heart was pounding like I had just been told by the coach that he wanted me to take the last shot in a basketball game and we were one point down. I actually had that opportunity against Whitthorne Junior High School a year earlier and shot an air ball. This shot that was coming up was more important than any basketball game. I went into 'the zone'.

I can still remember the feel of the string slipping through my fingers as I let it go. It had a different sensation than that of dropping a much lighter bird. I put the groundhog in the lap of the girl sitting in the passenger seat. This wasn't a great shot because I was aiming for the windshield. Everything went in slow motion after that.

If a dead groundhog lands in your lap, most will do just as she did. She did not immediately scream. I know sometimes things happen slower than we remember, but I am sure she just stared at it for about four seconds. She then screamed at the top of her lungs and jumped at the same time. I don't know how she got that much spring from a seated position, but she went straight up, which in turn threw the groundhog straight up in the air. While the groundhog was suspended in air, she jumped out of the Jeep. All heads turned towards her and then there were simultaneous screams from the rest of the girls.

The fact she jumped out was not too unexpected considering what had just landed in her lap. I don't want to take anything away from my shot, but in reality the Jeep was only traveling five or six miles per hour. She didn't even have to roll they were going so slow. She was able to land on her feet in a fast trot. I don't know where she was going, but she went from a trot to a sprint and headed around the Rayburn's house in full stride screaming at the top of her lungs and doing some kind of weird thing with her arms. The groundhog, which had gone airborne during this maneuver, landed back in the freshly emptied seat. The girls in the back followed suit and jumped out next. Still nothing earth shattering about that.

Then the driver jumped out. She didn't even touch the brakes. She just abandoned ship. Now this was totally unexpected. This was the downhill lane of the steep part of Washington Avenue. I never knew a driverless jeep with no foot on the accelerator could accelerate so fast.

It was one of those times that horseplay turned serious and I instantly regretted what I had done . . . mainly because I knew I was in big-time trouble. Once again, to keep from exaggerating here, the Jeep was probably only going fifteen miles per hour when it hit the big persimmon tree in the Jones' front yard, but it sounded like it hit much faster.

We all ran into the woods and watched from Rippey's Hill as parents arrived . . . ours and theirs. The police arrived also. Oh no, we were going to prison and I was only twelve. I knew my prints were on the string . . . and on the groundhog.

My parents acted as if they could not believe my sister and I had done such a thing. If my son did something like this today, I would also act appalled as if I would never have done such a thing as a child. The only thing that kept us from being grounded forever was the fact that they knew Hayes had a tendency to lead people astray, which we convinced them he had done in this case.

Paying for a jeep fender and radiator was not too bad in the late sixties when split between several sets of parents. Our young followers had to chip in too. We ratted them out. It only took me 6 months of mowing yards to pay my parents back. Mr. Hayes trimmed the fort/bush the next morning and I have never dropped a suspended animal from a power line since.

The Crash Test Dummy

Bobby Clark was another mastermind in the ways of pranks. His most classic prank occurred during a two week spell in which the temperature never rose above the freezing point. He had a life-size stuffed replica of the Mad Magazine character which happened to be about the size of a six year old kid. You older folks know the character I am talking about; the red headed guy with the stupid grin. He took the dummy, put it on a tricycle, and taped its feet and hands in place so it would look like a tricycle rider. He tried every way in the world to make the dummy's body stay upright on the tricycle, but it would slump over like it was dead. He tried bailing wire, rope, and twine, but nothing could make the dummy sit upright.

What he did next made us realize that he had more genius in him than Hayes. He took a garden hose and soaked the dummy with water. The genius then stood there for an hour shivering while holding the dummy in an upright position until it was frozen solid. It now sat upright on the tricycle with that stupid grin on its face.

The final touch of genius came when he ever so gently broke the ice away from the dummy's knees so its legs would move with the peddles when the tricycle was pushed.

Now he was ready. He waited by the evergreen bush in the Hayes' yard which had been trimmed back the previous summer, but was still large enough to cause a blind spot for a driver heading down Washington Avenue. He looked like a hunter waiting for game. He had a target in mind. He knew ole man Hildreth went to work about two o'clock in the afternoon. He let all other motorists pass. Then he heard the sound of ole man Hildreth's 62' Rambler fire up.

As the unsuspecting Mr. Hildreth came upon the bush, Bobby kicked the tricycle with his foot into the path of the Rambler. He had frozen the dummy's head so it stared directly to the left towards the oncoming vehicle. Nobody else in the world would have thought of that. It was if he was an artist and could envision what it would look like from the inside of a car. That smiling red headed dummy was looking at ole man Hildreth with that stupid grin as it peddled in front of his car. Mr. Hildreth had .15 of a second to react and hit his brakes.

It was an eerie sound. The squealing of the brakes, the crunch of the tricycle, then the sound of Mr. Hildreth screaming "Oh no" as he got out and crawled under his car to rescue what he was sure was a neighborhood child.

Some pictures in your mind will stay with you forever. Mr. Hildreth got up as if he were in slow motion. He slowly looked around to see who was responsible for this cruel act. Now that I am much older, I do realize it was a cruel act. As a kid, although not a delinquent myself but one that associated with delinquents, I thought it was a classic neighborhood moment. I was standing by Hayes' house about 50 feet away from the street with several other neighborhood kids laughing and pointing. Bobby was long gone into the woods . . . remember . . . he's a genius. I guess us innocent idiots figured ole man Hildreth would know we were just bystanders that thought it was funny.

Have you ever seen a giraffe run? I was at the Knoxville zoo and witnessed this happen one morning. They appear to be in slow motion. That is exactly what Mr. Hildreth looked like when he headed towards us. It was more of a lope, slowly changing to a serious sprint as he got his momentum up. Our faces changed from stupid grins to terror-filled faces. Instead of immediately running, we all looked at each other like they do in the movies, and then all bumped into each other and pushed off. Why do people do that? We then simultaneously ran for the woods. He could not catch us. What would he have done if he had? We had done a lot of stuff to him because we knew he had a bad temper, but I think this one had taken him over the edge.

When I got home, my dad was waiting. Now that I am a dad myself, I know he was disappointed in me even though I was truly an innocent bystander on this one. I also think that deep down inside he had to think to himself, "Whoever thought of this is a genius!" I had to go to my room for a few hours. He was more upset about Beth Brown's tricycle that was now a crumpled mess of scrap iron.

Mr. Brown was also furious about this. It only took us about a month to pay for it out of our allowances since there were five of us chipping in. We were now all mad at Clark for destroying the tricycle and costing us money. It was years later before I realized that this was one of the most classic pranks in the history of not only my town, but of all towns across the land.

I wonder if Bobby, now a preacher in Nashville, has ever told his congregation about this.

A Friend in Need

JUDGE ED RUNIONS was a World War II hero who had become a judge in my town. He got me and many others out of our share of traffic tickets when he felt we hadn't harmed society too much, and stuck us with some pretty hefty fines when he felt we had. This was standard practice in those days for most judges. He passed away a few years ago and is missed by our town and even more so by an increasingly complicated legal system.

I was awarded a ticket for doing seventy-five in a fifty-five mile per hour zone in Lewis County which is the county adjoining my county. I went to Judge Runions' office to see if he could help me out. He said he knew the judge in Lewis County and as a matter of fact, had recently helped two or three other people get out of tickets down there. He called the Lewis County judge as I sat in his office and said in his slow southern drawl, "Listen Judge, I have another friend here who got a ticket out on Highway 99 in your county and I was wondering if you could help him out?" I listened nervously as Judge Runions bobbed his head up and down and said, "Uh-huh, uh-huh, uh-huh, ok, talk to you later Judge" and hung up.

I said, "What did he say Judge?"

The Judge replied, "He told me I have too many friends."

I mailed sixty-eight dollars to the Lewis County Court Clerk the next day.

THE SPEEDING YANKEE

THE MOST MEMORABLE thing that ever happened in Judge Runions' courtroom occurred in the early sixties. An eyewitness was an older guy named Otis Benderman who gave me the details many years later while we sat and talked in a parking lot on The Z. Officer Manley Workman escorted a rough looking young gentleman from Indiana into the courthouse parking lot. The northerner was driving a souped-up 1955 Oldsmobile. Otis told me you could feel the ground rumble from the deep moan of the engine as he pulled in with Manley close behind in the squad car with siren blaring. As was usually the case, everyone in the courtroom knew everyone else . . . except no one knew this guy from way up north.

He was a stranger that had been passing through on Highway 43 heading home from somewhere south of Mount Pleasant. Manley interrupted the normal court proceedings and proudly paraded his catch up to the bench. A lawbreaker like this had to be dealt with immediately.

"Judge, this fella was heading north out by Hazel's Service Station and was driving at least eighty miles per hour in the forty-five mile per hour zone. It took me all the way to Zingarell's Market to get him stopped."

Judge Runions lowered his chin towards his chest, looked over his glasses at the northerner, and said, "I charge you with eighty miles per hour in a forty-five mile per hour zone. How do you plead?"

The perpetrator, showing great respect and standing at attention, responded, "I plead guilty your honor."

Judge Runions shuffled some papers around and said, "The fine will be fifty dollars young man."

The northerner reached into his wallet, pulled out a hundred dollar bill, and slapped it down on the judge's desk so hard it caused the gavel to fall over. "Here's a hundred . . . that'll cover my first fine and my second fine. I'm leaving this hillbilly town

13

the same way I came in!" He turned around and walked out without looking back.

The yankee's Oldsmobile was fishtailing as he squealed out of the parking lot in a cloud of smoke. Otis swears he was doing a hundred by the time he went over the hill on the northern edge of town. Everyone in the courtroom had jumped up from the old wooden church-style benches and had gathered at the large picture window that faced to the north. They were craning their necks as if they were watching a parade.

Manley jumped up and said, "I'll go get him Judge!" With that Manley darted towards the door.

Judge Runions calmly said, "Hold up Manley, he's paid his fine . . . next case."

THE LEGEND OF TOOTERBILL

THE MOST NOTORIOUS person in my home town was a fellow named Tooterbill Odom. I first heard of Tooterbill from one of his coworkers that frequented The Z. Tooterbill had a unique perspective on life and on his job.

Most people in my home town graduate from high school and go to work at Victor Chemical Corporation. They then work forty or so years and retire from Victor. There is nothing wrong with that. The plant provides good wages and a place people are proud to retire from. It has been like that since the twenties when the plant was built to process the rich reserves of phosphate buried in the ground around the county. My dad moved to Mount Pleasant from Nashville in the late 40's to go to work at Victor, so I guess you could say phosphate brought me to Mount Pleasant, even though I wasn't born yet when he made it to town.

Tooterbill worked at Victor and had an attendance problem. It seems he didn't like to work on Friday. After missing six Fridays in a row, the Human Resource Manager was able to determine a pattern had developed. He called Tooterbill onto the carpet to explain himself. The union representative accompanied Tooterbill to insure management did not trample on him.

The HR manager began the conversation with, "Tooterbill, you've worked four days a week for the last six weeks. Can you explain this pattern to me?"

Tooterbill reared back in his chair and rubbed his chin. After thirty seconds of deep thought he replied, "Well, I can't get by on just three days a week, so I work four."

The HR Manager bent his head forward, peaked over his half-lens reading glasses, and stared at Tooterbill for about ten seconds while digesting what he had just heard.

"That will be all Tooterbill." He dismissed Tooterbill, but asked the union representative to stay for a while so they could discuss Tooterbill's answer. Tooterbill evidently had not understood the point of the meeting.

Tooterbill eventually compromised with management after some pressure from the union rep and agreed to work three Fridays a month. Attendance was based on a point system and missing one Friday a month never accumulated enough points for termination, only a perpetual probation. Tooterbill did not mind being on perpetual probation.

The Greatest Fireworks Show on Earth

MOUNT PLEASANT BOASTED as being the phosphate capital of the world until the phosphate reserves ran out in the mid-eighties. The mines went dry. Victor management survived by being smart enough to begin processing other products that are hard to pronounce, but the huge ten story furnace building is in mothballs to this day. A chemical plant would normally not be thought of as beautiful, but to come over the hill and see this huge plant nestled in the holler (I will define holler in the next chapter) was a sight to see.

Phosphate looks like dirt when it is dug out of the ground. It was put into a huge furnace and heated to a thousand degrees or so. The phosphorous gas that was emitted from this process was captured through tubes and pipes at the top of the furnace resembling a huge whiskey still. As the phosphate was heated it also produced a combination of molten slag rock and iron as a bi-product. These bi-products had to be disposed of by 'tapping' the furnace before more phosphate could be added to get the next batch of high-dollar gas. Tapping basically meant opening a hole in the bottom of the furnace and draining out the stuff that looked like lava as it flowed out.

At night, the sky would turn bright orange as the furnace was tapped. I always wondered what a traveler passing through at night on Highway 43 thought this orange glow was. Whereas most people like to sit outside in the summertime and look at the stars, my father loved to sit outside on our back porch and watch the red glow of the western sky as the furnace was tapped every couple of hours.

The molten iron and slag were in layers inside the furnace like a mixture of oil and water. As the furnace was tapped, the molten slag rock came out first and was channeled using small clay dikes to a pit of water the size of a large pond so it could cool.

The molten iron, on the other hand, had to be channeled into a dry pit to be air cooled due to the fact that if you put molten metal into water it explodes. The problem was that they both came out of the same hole. When the color of the molten liquid changed from bright red to pale red as it came out of the hole, the highly trained workers knew the metal had begun coming out and they would quickly drop a square metal plate in the clay channel to reroute the molten metal down another channel into the dry pit far away from the water.

About once per year, an accident would occur and the molten metal would flow into the water instead of the dry pit. This caused a heck of an explosion known as a 'metal shot'. When the furnace operator saw that a metal shot was going to occur, he or she sounded an alarm and all of the plant workers scrambled inside concrete bunkers that were constructed throughout the plant for just such an occasion. Since they trained for this occurrence on a regular basis, injuries were rare during a metal shot.

When I was a child my family lived about five miles from the plant. On the one time or so a year that a metal shot occurred, it sounded like an atomic bomb had gone off outside of our house. The windows would rattle for a solid thirty seconds. When metal shots occurred at night, you could look towards the west and the sky would be filled with what appeared to be a hundred small campfires that had been flung hundreds of feet into the air floating in slow motion back towards earth. Each of these small balls of fire had a comet like tail streaking from behind.

One Fourth of July in the late seventies, Tooterbill happened to be working the evening shift. That, in and of itself, was not too bad. Since it was the Fourth of July, all of the bosses had the day off and Tooterbill was working unsupervised. That was bad any day of the year. Approximately nine o'clock, as most other townsfolk were gathered at the city park awaiting the city fireworks show, Tooterbill was simultaneously routing the molten metal purposefully into the pit of water that was the last place on earth the molten metal needed to go.

He had carefully timed it to coincide with the nine o'clock fireworks show. He was kind enough to sound the alarm so the rest of the unsuspecting plant workers could scramble to the bunkers. Just as the high-priced fireworks show that Mayor Boyd had arranged began at the park, the earth shook. Every local in the park knew what the sound was and looked west. The people who had come from out of town all snatched their heads down like a pack of turtles going into their shells. The sky to the west lit up 'like the Fourth of July' (excuse the pun). The city fireworks continued to the east and Tooterbill's fireworks were to the west. It was a beautiful site.

As Tooterbill and the union rep sat in the HR manager's office the next day, the manager showed them on paper that Tooterbill's fireworks show was much more expensive than the city fireworks show after considering cleanup costs, plant downtime, and the time it took managers to write reports to other managers about what went wrong.

Tooterbill's assurance that it was an accident and his denial of circumstantial evidence such as the precise timing of the accident got him off the carpet with a warning. He had to work an extra Friday a month for a few months to balance out his perpetual probation since he had accumulated new points from the warning, but he was never scheduled to work another 'bossless' holiday.

HOLLER: I.E.-A CONCAVE AREA BETWEEN HILLS

ANY OF THE small unincorporated communities scattered around the rolling hills of my county are named after the holler in which they are nestled in. You have Pickard Holler, Sheepneck Holler, Blowing Springs Holler, and many more. I even lived 'up in a holler', but it didn't have enough population to have a name.

When my daughter Jessica began the second grade, she had a teacher from up north. She was a great teacher, but talked funny. One night Jessica was sitting on my lap as she read me a story. She read aloud, "And the villain went between the hills into the hollow . . ." She pronounced holler as if it ended with a long O sound. It sounded more like hollow. Just because it is spelled like that doesn't mean you pronounce it like that!

"Wooohhhh", I exclaimed. "What did you just say?"

She repeated, "And the villain went between the hills into the hollow . . ."

I stopped her again. "Who taught you how to say holler like that?"

"Mrs. Patterson", she explained.

"Well never let me here you saw that again! H-O-L-L-O-W (I spelled it out for her) is pronounced holler in Tennessee girl . . . I repeat . . . H-O-L-L-0-W . . . holler. Never forget that!"

I think I caught her just in time before the damage was done. To this day as educated as my daughter is and as good as she is at enunciating her words, she will still talk about the 'holler' that she grew up in. That's my girl!

THE GATE KEEPERS OF PICKARD HOLLER

OU WOULD NOT think that a couple of farm kids opening a gate would be legendary, but neighbors witnessing this ritual soon spread the word enough for the tradition to make county legend status. Fred Russell lived about five miles west of Mount Pleasant near Hampshire.

I played basketball against Hampshire in high school. Their gymnasium was actually a converted tobacco barn with a hardwood floor and bleachers made of pine boxes. If you arched your shot too much, it would hit the rafters. Make no mistake, they could play some ball down there and probably had the best home court advantage in the state . . . maybe in the country.

The Russells lived in Pickard Holler just before you got to Hampshire in an old white farmhouse. There was a gate at the beginning of their long driveway to keep the livestock from wandering onto Pickard Holler Road. Fred had trained his kids to run and open the gate upon hearing the sound of his horn as he drove up the holler towards his driveway. Failing to get to the gate and have it opened before Fred turned into the drive meant a sure whipping (that means a spanking for you folks raised in the city). After all, that would mean Fred would actually have to get out of the truck to open it himself.

People who saw the ritual said it was like a fire drill. When Fred turned off of Hampshire pike onto the dirt road that headed up Pickard Holler, he would begin sounding his horn. Two kids would immediately burst out of the front screen door of the house and leap from the wooden front porch in full stride towards the gate. It was about the length of a football field from the house. They only had about twenty seconds to get it open once they heard the horn or they were sure to face corporal punishment. They would open the gate, stand at a semi-attention as he pulled through, and then close the gate before any livestock could get out. Fred would pull through without having to slow down and head up the driveway in his old rusted out 52' GMC pickup truck.

The kids eventually moved away, but before they left they gave their dad the best Father's day gift a dad could want. They had a concrete cattle gap installed at the gate that would keep the cows in the field without having to close the gate each time. I believe Fred would have sold his cows or adopted more kids before he had to stoop to having to open the gate himself and would certainly have never spent 300 bucks on a cattle gap himself.

THE HOMING MULE

WHAT IS THE only animal on the face of the earth that could go extinct, yet could become unextinct (if there is such a word) in about a year? A mule! All mules are sterile. A mule is the product of a male donkey and a female horse, so a mule is not required to produce a baby mule.

Maury County Tennessee, the county where Mount Pleasant is located, boasts of being the mule capital of the world. Each year, the first weekend of April is the Mule Day Celebration. Columbia, the county seat, swells from fifty thousand or so people to about two hundred thousand. Mules and their owners arrive from all over the country. People all over America take their mules seriously. Out of all the mules that come to town on this weekend, no mule story has ever topped what a team of mules belonging to Isaiah Boshears had become famous for years earlier. Make no mistake, mules are pretty smart creatures.

Back in the early sixties, the Mount Pleasant town square was a crowded place each Saturday night. The farmers would hitch up their mules and take their wagons to town while the town folk (those that didn't own a mule) would either walk or drive their cars 'uptown'. I can remember my dad putting my brother, my two sisters, and me in the bed of his pickup truck in the summer and heading to town. Mule wagons would be parked everywhere. You also had to watch where you stepped. Olean's Pool Hall would be the most crowded spot in town.

Isaiah drank a little too much whiskey on a regular basis. Dr. Williams had told him his drinking was going to kill him, but Isaiah insisted he could not completely quit. Dr. Williams, trying to be compassionate, had come up with a reasonable compromise. He cut Isaiah down to one shot glass of whiskey per day. Isaiah agreed, but figured out a little different schedule. He figured he could go all week without drinking, then drink seven shots of whiskey each Saturday night. This still averaged 1 shot per day.

Isaiah would get drunk in the pool room and pass out every Saturday night. Some of his buddies would put him in the bed of his wagon, slap his mules on the rear, and watch them make a slow u-turn on Main Street and then meander off into the dark as they headed the five or so miles back to Watts Hill on the south end of the county. They would actually take him home and stop in front of his house. Martha, Isaiah's wife, would hear the mules' hooves clambering on the hard-packed dirt road as they approached the house. She would go out and put a blanket on him in the summertime or call her son to help get him inside in the winter.

Isaiah finally quit drinking later in life, but would still come to town on Saturday night. It's a good thing he stayed sober because he outlived his legendary mules and his new mules had to be guided home each Saturday night.

THE MULE TRADER

ONE OF THE major events of Mule Day Weekend to this day is trading livestock and accessories. I have a buddy that thinks he is the best trader in the state, but is probably the worst. If you were to witness him trading, you would think he is among the best. He talks a good game. At the end of the day, his results usually indicate he is among the worst. This particular day I saw him by Lucille's Restaurant just off of the town Square in Columbia. He had his team of mules with him that he had owned for a few years, two nice leather yokes, and a wagon. He was grinning like a possum eating saw briar (I know . . . actually opossum) when he showed me what he was going to be trading. I wished him luck and proceeded out to Maury County Park to see the tobacco spitting contest.

Have you ever witnessed a possum eating saw brier? Saw brier is encased in stickers, so the possum has to curl its lips back to eat it. Nobody has ever completely witnessed a possum finish eating it because seeing this always brings out a loud cackle which scares the possum away.

Late that afternoon, I went back to the courthouse square where the trading was going on just in time to see my buddy trading for a team of mules. I guess most mules look similar, but these mules sure looked very familiar to me. It turns out that at the end of the trading day, he traded back for the same team of mules he had started with that morning but had traded away earlier in the day. His yokes and his wagon had also been traded away and were gone. What a skilled trader. He started with several items and ended up with only the same mules he started with.

THE LUCKIEST THIEF IN THE EAST

S TRETCH PRUITT, ANOTHER local legend, was most famous for his dirt track antics. He could take a stock camshaft, build it up with a welder, and then turn it into a high rise camshaft with a metal file in order to get more horsepower out of his engine. If they tore his engine down at the dirt strip to verify his engine didn't have an illegal high rise camshaft, the part number on the cam shaft would match the stock camshaft part number at Wimp's Auto Parts where all of the verifications were done. He got away with this for years until somebody finally decided to actually measure the lobes on the shaft. They just didn't look right. He was busted.

Stretch owned a little convenience store in a converted gas station just outside of town. I stopped there one hot day to get something cold to drink. The regular patrons that hung out at his store were normally sitting on a bench next to the beer cooler telling tall tales. This particular day they were in the candy aisle wearing welding gloves and tossing a live rattlesnake back and forth. They were keeping score, but I didn't know the rules and didn't care who was winning. I decided to ease on back to my pickup truck and grab a cold drink at the next store.

A couple of weeks later I stopped in to get a drink and asked Stretch if he still had the pet rattlesnake. He reared back in his chair and proudly told me what he had done with the snake.

It seems somebody had been breaking into his soft drink machine located on the outside of his store. They would pry the machine open and empty the change box in the middle of the night. It was happening two or three nights a week. Stretch had come upon the rattler on his farm and had an instant epiphany. He didn't know he had had one of those, but that is exactly what had happened.

He had fixed a similar problem with a thief earlier in the year. He kept a delivery van parked at his store and somebody would steal the battery out of it each weekend. He cut the end off of an extension cord, hooked 110 volts up to each post of the battery, and plugged it in. When he came in to work Monday morning, the hood was up on the van, but the battery was still there. Somebody got jolted. His battery has not been stolen since. Word travels fast in a small town.

He had thought about trying that same trick with the drink machine but had feared he would electrocute an innocent person who was merely thirsty or electrocute himself if he got thirsty and forgot it was wired. He decided to use the snake to catch the thief. Stretch unlocked the machine, removed the change box, and carefully used welding gloves to put the snake behind the box so that anyone putting their hand near the box would get a shock . . . not an electric one. He then replaced the change box which kept the snake in place behind the box and locked the machine with the snake inside.

When Stretch arrived at the store the next morning, the door of the drink machine had been pried open and the change box was lying beside the open door. All the money was still in the box. The snake was gone.

Thad Kelly was treated for a rattlesnake bite on his hand at Maury County hospital about three in the morning. He said he had been bitten while in his barn feeding his chickens. Nobody ever broke into Stretch's drink machine again. As stated before, word travels fast in a small town.

THE HATBAND

I READ IN THE paper one time that someone had put a rattlesnake in a judge's mailbox for revenge. I have not stuck my hand in my mailbox after dark since without first shining a flashlight into the hole. I am not a judge, but people make mistakes. I am only afraid of four kinds of snakes . . . big ones, little ones, live ones, and dead ones.

Southern Maury County Tennessee has a large rattlesnake population. Legend has it that back in the fifties railroad workers had to wear stove pipes on their lower legs to keep from getting snake bit while cleaning up a train derailment on the south end of the county.

A buddy of mine rolled into work one morning and shut his truck off as it coasted to a stop. He was ghost-white pale. When I asked him what was wrong, he told me of an encounter with one of these slimy beasts that occurred a few minutes earlier. As he was driving to work he saw a five-foot Diamond Back Rattler crossing the road. All he could think was 'oh boy, a hatband'. He squealed to a stop and grabbed his shotgun out of the gun rack of his four-wheel drive pickup. As the viper crawled up the bank on the side of the road, my buddy eased up close enough to shoot the snake's head off at close range. He didn't want to shoot from a distance for fear that the shotgun pellets would ruin his new hatband.

Have you ever touched a snake after it was dead? My dad showed me what a dead snake could do when I was a boy. For an hour or so after a snake dies it will still react when you touch it (verify this if you want to). The nerve endings in the skin make it move as if it were still alive.

My buddy was one of those guys that always wore combat fatigues and kept a big pocket knife in a leather case strapped to his belt. After shooting the snake's head off, Mike took his knife out, straddled his hat band, and put his foot on the snake in order to start the skinning process. He simultaneously moved

28

his hand into position to grip the dead snake. Just as his hand was over the snake, the stump where the head used to be reared back and struck his wrist hard enough to knock the knife out of his hand. This big, tough guy told me he jumped backwards, fell on his rear end, and rolled away from the snake. He said some kind of weird whimpering noise came out of his mouth involuntarily as he rolled.

After he knew he was a safe distance from the snake, he tried to stand up. His legs would not support the weight of his body. The next thing he did was check his pulse. His heart was beating over 200 beats per minute. It was more like a hum than a fast beat. His biggest fear now was having a heart attack. He could not catch his breath. He knew the snake was dead, but it had still scared the heck out of him.

When he finally managed to stand up and get in his truck, he could not push the clutch in to put the truck in gear. When he would attempt to push it in, his foot would just quiver rather than push. He finally had to crank his truck while it was in gear. It snatched his neck pretty good, but fired up allowing him to drive to work slowly in first gear.

I asked him where the snake was now. He told me it was still lying on the bank with its head shot off and I could have it if I wanted it. I did not take him up on his offer. I let the buzzards have the hatband.

A Hole in the Earth

When I was a boy, my mother told me that if I dug far enough in our backyard I would eventually reach China. This was theoretically true, but I don't think she meant for me to try it. The next day, I enlisted the help of several neighborhood kids and we headed to China by digging under the big Mulberry tree beside our porch using spoons swindled from each of our kitchens. We should have picked a spot with no roots, but eight year olds don't anticipate such things.

This memory was the first thing that came to my mind when I heard what happened to Earl Russell one cool spring night. My oldest sister, Mary Anna, was a senior at Hay Long High School in Mount Pleasant. The year was 1969. A popular hangout for the teenagers at the time was the fire tower about five miles east of Mount Pleasant. This particular night would end in near tragedy.

The fire tower was located in a pine thicket. Thank God for the soft padding of pine needles that had accumulated on the ground under these huge pine trees through the years. Earl had become known for his climbing ability while hanging tobacco at various barns around the county. If you have ever been unfortunate enough to have to hang tobacco at harvest time, you know the person on the top row does half as much work as the person on the bottom row, so a race for the top row is a tradition at tobacco hanging time. Earl was usually the first one to the top.

After a night of standing around the campfire at the fire tower, Earl decided to show off his climbing prowess. He climbed to the top of the fire tower, not using the steps, but using the outside steel girders. The girls were truly impressed. The problem occurred when he was climbing back down. Most fire towers in the south are in a pine thicket. Back in the forties and fifties when they built these towers they would clear the ground, build the tower, and then plant a pine tree every eight feet or so all around the property. After twenty years or so, these trees had grown up about half as tall as the fire tower. Since the trees were all planted at the same time, they grew at pretty close to the same rate and after twenty years all were close to the same height.

When Earl started his climb back down, it seemed to him he had been descending for quite some time. When he got about four feet above the top of the level growth of pine trees, he thought he was four feet above the ground. In the darkness, the tops of the trees in the evenly-grown thicket looked like dark, level ground to him. The thick treetops did not let the campfire that was on the real ground shine through. He stepped off of the fire tower four feet above the treetops, which was about forty feet above the ground.

My sister recalled that it took him twenty seconds or so to get all the way to the ground. He hit every limb of one of the pine trees on the way down and landed with a thud. They put him in the back of Johnny Whitwell's pickup truck and headed to Maury County Hospital.

The next day he was recovering from a broken leg and a heck of a hangover. He said he thought he had fallen through the earth. He said just before he stepped off of the tower, he wondered why the campfire had been put out and everybody had left the party.

A Penny for your Thoughts

ONE OF THE main hangouts in town was the Gulf Station on Main Street. Main Street was on the return trip as a traveler along The Z meandered from the end of Fairview Drive back to Zingarell's Market. This was a typical old fashioned gas station with the gas pumps on the outside and a two bay garage that usually had a car raised up on the lift inside. The business closed at 6pm nightly and shortly thereafter the tailgaters would arrive. I spent many nights there myself watching the traffic go by.

One muggy Saturday night, a bunch of us hillbillies were sitting around chewing the fat when blue lights appeared on the hill near the town square. The lights were trailing a motorcycle that eventually pulled into the Gulf Station about fifteen feet from where we were gathered. When the rider took his helmet off we could see it was Tooterbill. Tooterbill liked an audience which he now had. This was not your ordinary traffic stop. Instead of the Mount Pleasant Police Department, it was a Tennessee State Trooper. We didn't see state troopers inside the city limits very often, but it turns out this trooper had been chasing Tooterbill all the way from Hazel's Service Station which was about a mile south of the city limits.

The trooper had just begun writing the ticket when Tooterbill cut his eyes at us to make sure we were looking and said, "Sir, what would you do if I called you a bigheaded idiot?" That got a cackle out of us which made Tooterbill bow his shoulders back a little bit and slightly cock his head to the side.

The trooper stopped writing, looked at Tooterbill for a few seconds, and said, "If you called me a bigheaded idiot I would put you in the back of my squad car and take you to jail!" The trooper continued with a five second intimidating stare at Tooterbill, then slowly put his head back down and started writing again, shaking his head in unbelief that this hick had asked such a question.

I could tell Tooterbill's mind was whirling. He scratched his chin like Sherlock Holmes must have done when pondering a mystery and said, "Sir, what would you do if I just *thought* you were a bigheaded idiot?"

The trooper, who did happen to have a big head, stopped writing. He continued staring at the ticket book as he pondered this question posed to him by the philosophical Tooterbill. After fifteen seconds of silence, he looked up slowly at Tooterbill who appeared to really want an answer to this loophole he had come up with. After all, a person can *think* anything he wants.

The officer actually put his finger on his cheek and stared toward the sky as he answered the question, "Well son, if you just *thought* I was a bigheaded idiot there wouldn't be much I could do about that, now would there!" He gave Tooterbill another mean stare of ten seconds or so, and then shook his head and went back to writing.

I don't know if Tooterbill truly thought he had a loophole or if he couldn't stand a chance to go down in history, but he said, "Well then I *THINK* you are a bigheaded idiot."

We all started laughing and slapping our legs which didn't help matters. He definitely made history. I will never forget him looking back at us out of the back window and grinning as the trooper, who had put him in the back of the patrol car as he said he would, headed north towards Maury County Jail. Tooterbill had acted shocked that the officer had arrested him and kept repeating, "But you said I could think it, you said I could think it!" He was still looking back at us as they went over the north horizon.

About fifteen minutes later, Blackie's Wrecker Service hooked to the motorcycle and took it over the south horizon towards the city impound lot.

THE DEMOLITION DERBY

VERY LABOR DAY weekend the Maury County Fair cranks up at the fairgrounds. This particular year the fair coincided with the final court date of a nasty divorce between Gene Vandigriff and his wife Charlene. Gene only had one possession that he wanted to keep. They had bought a brand new Malibu at Lucas Chevrolet a year earlier. Unfortunately for Gene, the judge awarded Charlene the house, the furniture, the cows, the chickens, and the Malibu. He was ordered to have the car parked in her driveway by the end of the Labor Day weekend, specifically by eight o'clock Tuesday morning.

One of the main events of the fair each year was the Demolition Derby. Teams of wannabe NASCAR drivers would go out to Blackie's junk yard 6 months before the fair came to town and buy a junk car that was still drivable and start knocking out the glass and welding reinforcement beams on the doors.

If you have never seen a demolition derby, they basically line up twenty or so old cars on a dirt field, fire a pistol to start the derby, and the drivers start running into each other just like bumper cars. For safety's sake, all windows of the cars are knocked out and the gas tanks are replaced by one gallon safety tanks so the drivers don't blow each other up. One gallon is enough to power the vehicles for the fifteen minutes or so that it takes to make all but one vehicle inoperable. The last car able to move takes the trophy home.

The judge's ruling came on Friday afternoon. Gene was a regular at the derby in years past, but had not planned on entering this year since cash was tight during this ugly divorce. A thought came to him within seconds of the judge's ruling, "You know, the judge said to give her the car back, but he didn't mention what kind of shape it had to be in when I give it back." Gene had figured out a loophole in the ruling. He even took the time to read the order in detail to make sure there was nothing in there about the condition of the car. Later that night he took a

34

sledge hammer and began knocking the glass out of his car that would be Charlene's car Tuesday morning. He went to Rippey's Auto Parts and bought a safety tank to replace the twenty gallon gas tank.

All of the other contestants had twenty year old faded, rusted vehicles when they lined up at the fairgrounds 8pm Saturday night. Gene's car stood out as the crowd began pointing at the shiny late-model windowless Malibu with the number eight spray painted on each door.

When the pistol fired, Gene was the clear front runner. He had forgotten about the air bag in this state of the art vehicle, so he was jolted pretty good on his first impact. It only stayed inflated for a couple of seconds, so as he came out of his disorientation he could see again. He had to breathe the fumes emitted from the deployment of the bag for another twenty seconds or so, but he was beginning to breathe dust from the dirt track anyway. After he got his bearings, the late-model car was no match for the older cars. He got hit at least once by every car in the event, but in the end he was the last car deemed drivable by the event judge. Gene had won the Maury County Demolition Derby.

When he drove the car into Charlene's driveway on Tuesday morning, it looked like a twenty year old beat up car from Blackie's junk yard. He had reinstalled the factory gas tank and saved the one gallon safety tank for next year's derby car. He left the trophy in the front seat, the keys in the ignition, and walked the three blocks back to his house.

It turns out there was some obscure law on the books about the intent of your actions when turning over property in a divorce settlement. Gene spent Tuesday night in Maury County Jail, was bailed out Wednesday morning by his brother, and on the advice of his attorney went to Lucas Chevrolet and purchased a one year old Malibu with intact windows for his ex-wife. He did get to keep the beat up Malibu, so he already had next year's derby car.

THE ENGINEERING STUDENTS

My DAD WAS a mechanical engineer and a graduate of Vanderbilt University. He was the smartest man I ever knew. Most people around our town who knew my dad would agree with that statement. When my younger brother and I were thirteen and fifteen respectively, my dad decided to teach us how to survey with an engineering transit. You've seen the people on the highway with the orange vests looking through the small telescope-like instrument and a guy about a hundred yards away holding a ten foot tall stick with numbers on it. Well, that was me and bro.

We both had fair book sense, but had both repeatedly done some pretty stupid things in our years on the earth. Our dad had witnessed many of these things or received phone calls about them, so he knew he had a tedious task to teach us anything. Most people around our town who know my brother and me would agree with that statement also.

The object is to look through the magnifying lens of the transit, which is perfectly level, and record the number you see on the stick that is being held by the other person so people can build level stuff such as roads and bridges. In order to train us, my dad would look through the lens first and write the number down. He would curl his hand around the pencil and paper as he wrote so his short-cut taking sons would not just repeat the number they saw him write down. He would then let his students look through the lens and report the number we saw to him so he could make sure we were reading the same number and thus reading the instrument correctly.

I peered through the instrument first while my brother held the stick about the length of a football field away. I got within a half inch or so which would never have gotten me through engineering school, but satisfied my dad. When it came my brothers turn, I walked the hundred or so yards to hold the

36

measuring stick so my brother could get prepared to build roads, bridges, or space ships.

My brother would look through the lens and tell dad the number, which should match the number my dad had just recorded. I would see my dad flailing his arms, and then push his illiterate son out of the way and look through the lens again to make sure the transit had not been knocked off level. He would then demand my brother look again to see the number he should have seen the first time. The big old dumb boy would be two inches off this time also.

What they did not know was that when my father would look, I would have the measuring stick on the ground where it should be. When he would step back and let my brother look, it gave me just enough time to lift the measuring stick onto the toe of my boot. The 2 inches from the ground to the toe of my boot was enough to befuddle the best of engineers and cause total chaos a football field away from me. When my father would take his second look, I would ease the stick back onto the ground. I would let my brother get it right each third look, either because I had a heart or because I knew my dad would figure out that his dumbest son was doing something to cause this if it went on too long.

My brother David is now a successful engineer in Nashville. I did not help him get there. I am not an engineer.

All You Can Eat

OTT JONES HAD gained notoriety around the county for being a shrewd dealer in the used automobile trade. Ott weighed in at just under four hundred pounds and was more famous for his ability to eat and drink than selling cars. He ate cheeseburgers by the half dozen and Pabst Blue Ribbon beer by the quart.

One night a crew of seven or eight people had gone over to West Tennessee to the Thursday night auto auction in Henry County. About halfway back to Mount Pleasant they came across a catfish restaurant on the bank of Tennessee River that had a portable sign by the edge of the highway that read, "All you can eat Catfish-eight bucks". They pulled in, got a table, and started eating. Everyone at the table had eaten a couple of plates of catfish, had pushed their plates away, and were now chewing on toothpicks and watching Ott. He was on his fifth plate of fish and showed no sign of slowing down. He was knocking a plate out every sixty seconds or so.

A very concerned manager, who had to feed the local population for the rest of the night, approached the table and told my friend Buzz, "If all of you will walk out right now and take this fella with you, none of you owe us a dime!"

Ott slid the last fish through his teeth leaving nothing but bones and the tail, belched, wadded his napkin up in his plate, got up and left. You could see catfish bones in his teeth as he smiled on the way out of the door.

They stepped into a convenience store and bought Ott five packs of peanut butter crackers and two quarts of Pabst Blue Ribbon to sustain him as they headed back across the river towards Mount Pleasant.

THE TWICE CONSUMED
MELLOW YELLOW

JIMMY ADAMS WORKED at Victor. He despised bums. He chewed Red Man tobacco and kept his unchewed pouch in his right back pocket. In his left back pocket he kept a pouch of his already chewed tobacco that he would deposit in the bag when it ran out of flavor. When someone asked to bum a chew, they got their pull from the pouch in his left back pocket. Nobody ever asked him for a chew twice, although they probably didn't know they were chewing 'already been chewed' tobacco. They just figured he had low grade tobacco.

The problem Jimmy was experiencing at work was not related to tobacco, but was bum related. Jimmy kept a one liter bottle of Mellow Yellow in the break room refrigerator for lunch and breaks. He started noticing that someone was consuming his favorite soft drink when he wasn't around. He would lose a couple of inches of drink each day. Jimmy decided to spend a day in the lab which was next door to the break room. His supervisor cleared him to do this after Jimmy told him the reason. Stealing a person's food or drink from the company fridge was the equivalent of horse thievery in the 1800's. Jimmy cracked the lab door just enough to see into the break room but not be noticed. He set up position at an angle that gave him a clear view of the refrigerator.

It only took until the morning break to catch the culprit. He witnessed Odell Watkins open the refrigerator, look around like a kid about to steal gum from the candy rack, and poor a glass full of Mellow Yellow from Jimmy's bottle. Jimmy watched and waited until Odell had finished drinking the stolen substance, then made his entrance.

Jimmy went to the refrigerator, unscrewed the cap of his bottle of Mellow Yellow, turned it up and took a mouthful straight from the bottle. He reared his head back and did his best gargle with the mouthful of yellow soft drink just as one would do with mouthwash. He had bubbles erupting from his mouth like a rabid dog. He then swished the drink around in his mouth making sure it swirled through the gaps in his tobacco stained teeth, put his mouth back over the opening of the Mellow Yellow bottle, and spit the mouth rinse back into the bottle. He twisted the cap back on, put the bottle back in the refrigerator, and headed nonchalantly towards the door.

"What in the world did you just do?" asked Odell as his face was changing to a slight shade of green.

Jimmy replied, "Oh, I just use that bottle to rinse my mouth after I get finished with a chew of tobacco." Jimmy had never actually offered anyone a chew of tobacco before, but felt it was appropriate to offer Odell a chew. Odell after all looked like he needed something to sterilize his mouth. "Do you want a chew of my Red Man Odell?"

"Yea, I think I do!" was the grossed out Odell's response to his offer. Jimmy pulled the pouch out of his left back pocket and gave Odell a pull. Jimmy has not had a problem with missing Mellow Yellow since and Odell never asked him for another chew of tobacco.

THE BODY MAN

EVERY COMMUNITY HAS a person that is famous for being the best bondo and paint specialist in the town. My town is no different. Have you noticed that most great body shop owners are also unique characters? We had a person on the south end of town that could take a total wreck and make it look like a new vehicle in just a few days. He was also known to participate in insurance fraud on occasions. He will remain unnamed since the statute of limitations is a little gray here.

On this particular occasion, a gentleman that owned a Volkswagen bug had blown the engine during a high speed jaunt from Columbia to Mount Pleasant. High speed in a Volkswagen would only get you a ticket in a school zone, but he had managed to wind the engine tight enough to blow it. He went to see the unnamed body repairman since he did not have the money to buy a new engine. He knew that this person had a 20 foot cliff in the holler behind his shop that had seen more cars plummet off of it than all scenes in every James Bond movie combined. He would just total the car out, collect the insurance, and buy a car with a good engine.

Most cases of insurance fraud don't get well publicized, but in this case word got out fast and it went down in county history. The repairman/future felon pulled the VW around to the top of the cliff with his wrecker, and then pushed the VW off the cliff. The VW amazingly did a full flip on the way down and landed on its wheels in an upright position like a cat does when you hold it upside down and drop it from chest high (not that I have ever done that).

The perpetrator scratched his head, and then drove his wrecker to the bottom to retrieve the barely damaged car so he could repeat the exercise. It unbelievably happened again! The VW did a complete flip and landed on its wheels! Yes-he did it a third time and had the same result. He knew he didn't have access to a cliff of a different height, so he had to deviate from his normal process of totaling a vehicle for insurance purposes.

In the end he had to take a 16 pound sledge hammer and beat on the car until he reached the point that any legitimate insurance adjuster would consider the vehicle totaled. He did such a good job the only comment the adjuster had for the vehicle owner was, "It's a miracle you lived through that!"

"It is indeed a miracle. I walked away without a scratch" was the only retort the owner could think of as he received his check for the totaled VW. This particular body shop owner eventually spent eighteen months at Brushy Mountain State Prison for helping a Tennessee Bureau of Investigation agent total his car, but has never been charged for the VW incident.

YOU GET WHAT YOU PAY FOR

OWN THE ROAD from this unnamed body repairman was another body shop owned by Randy Giles. He usually did honest work, but if you made him mad he tended to be spiteful. He was the type of person that would look you in the eye and tell you if he pulled one over on you. He didn't keep it a secret because he never cheated anybody that didn't deserve it.

A gentleman that was known to be rather wealthy around the county stopped in one day to get an estimate on his Cadillac. He had hit a pole at the American Legion Club on Saturday night and the left front fender had a severe dent. Randy told him it would run him about three hundred bucks to fix it. The wealthy gentleman then insulted Randy by telling him he could get it fixed across town for half that price. Instead of telling him where to go . . . across town of course, Randy said, "Well then, I can fix it for a hundred dollars." All you could see was teeth as the grinning Cadillac owner left his car with Randy to be repaired.

If you don't know anything about doing body work, bondo is the fiberglass material they use to fill holes and dents on the body of a car. It is similar in texture to spackle or joint compound used for home repair. If the dent is too deep, the fender must be replaced because the bondo is not designed to use in anything dented deeper than an inch or so. If the dent is deeper than an inch, it can sometimes be 'beat out' with a hammer from the other side to bring it out to within the one inch deep rule of thumb. If there is any metal that cannot be beat back out to within an inch of the original fender, it should be replaced.

Randy's original intention was to replace the fender when he gave the three hundred dollar quote. The fender was dented in a good eight inches. After the insult, Randy decided to use bondo instead. Randy went into the shop, mixed up a gallon container of bondo, and slapped it into the dented fender just as it was . . . an eight inch dent. He should have at least sanded away the crinkled paint before applying bondo so it would stick to the metal, but there was no time to do that on a hundred dollar job.

After a couple of hours, the bondo had dried. After sanding the fender into shape, Randy should have then put a coat of primer on the fresh bondo so the paint would stick longer than a week. He instead skipped that step and painted right over the fresh bondo. He made it look like a new fender with his craftsmanship and shiny paint.

He could not afford new Chrome since this was a hundred dollar job, so he took all of the chrome from the right side of the car and moved it to the left side of the car to replace the damaged left side chrome. The left hub cap had also been destroyed, so Randy replaced it with the hub cap from the right side.

The next day, the Cadillac owner showed up to get his car. Randy had parked it next to a large hedge bush so the Cadillac owner could not see the right side of the car that had been stripped down so the left side would look good. The owner was all teeth again as he examined this excellent body work. He left and headed north on Highway 43.

He returned about three hours later. You could see no teeth and his face was as red as an ape's rear end. The dried gallon of beautifully crafted bondo had simply fallen off in a solid chunk as he drove down Main Street. It was too heavy and had nothing to stick to but old chipped paint. When he pulled over to see what had fallen off, he noticed the right side was missing all of its chrome parts.

Randy told the Cadillac owner, "You wanted a hundred dollar job, you got a hundred dollar job. If you want it fixed right, it'll be three hundred dollars!"

Judge Runions made Randy give the Cadillac owner his hundred dollars back. Randy argued that the Cadillac owner should at least pay for the gallon of bondo, but the judge didn't agree. The Cadillac owner went to the other side of town to get his car repaired the correct way.

THE CHAMPION DUCK DOG

WHEN I WAS seven years old, my dad hung out with Uncle Alan Hardison and Cotton Rippey. The latter two had taken up bird hunting. Quail season had ended, so both of them had spent hard earned money on Labrador Retrievers to get ready for duck season. Well, my dad wasn't going to be outdone. He loaded my little brother and me up in his pickup truck and we headed 50 miles north to Nashville to buy a dog he had found in the Nashville Banner classifieds. This Black Lab pup's father was some kind of Canadian duck hunting champion and its mother also had a pretty powerful pedigree according to the seller.

I don't know the denomination of the bills my dad shucked out, but he looked like he was dealing a poker hand to a full table. We headed back home and for the next month or so Uncle Alan, Cotton, and dear ole Dad trained these high-dollar dogs in Uncle Alan's back yard. They had purchased a book that came with plastic ducks and a little horn that sounded like a duck quacking.

Victor Chemical was surrounded by twenty or so huge man-made lakes that were referred to as mud ponds. They used these lakes to have a place to pump the dirt that was washed off of the phosphate ore. Since these lakes were constructed over forty years ago and had been filled with this discarded dirt, they had become shallow lakes and were mostly overgrown with cattails and willow trees. This was perfect duck hunting territory. The first day of duck season, my dad woke me before dawn. We met Uncle Alan and Cotton at one of the mud ponds, unloaded the dogs, loaded our shotguns, and started splashing through ankle deep water towards a clearing to wait on flying ducks.

Cotton Rippey had a brand new pickup truck. It was shiny and green. The mistake he made this morning was leaving the passenger side window down while he splashed through the water with us. We were about the length of a football field from his truck, but from where I was standing it was clearly visible. We were at the edge of the woods where the water had become deep enough that Willow trees no longer grew. The water became an actual lake at this point rather than a swamp.

I will never forget hearing the shots ring out and watching two ducks splash into the water about twenty yards in front of me. I couldn't wait to see how my hunting dog measured up. Uncle Alan's dog and Cotton's dog busted the water in full stride. It is a beautiful sight watching good retrievers at work.

My champion duck dog was running much faster than the other dogs, but he was going in the other direction. One of those greyhound racing dogs could not have beaten him back to the parking area. He looked like a black streak as he bolted down the path and took a long leap towards the open window of Cotton's truck.

He got his front paws curled over the partially rolled down window and seemed to hang there for a few seconds. He then started pushing off of the side of the shiny green door with his back feet and claws as he tried to climb into the opening. He looked like a cartoon character as his legs were moving in a full stride, but he was going nowhere. The sound of his claws digging in the side of Cotton's truck was reminiscent of Cabbagehead Floyd scraping his fingernails down the blackboard in our 2nd grade class.

My dog finally created enough friction with his back feet to propel his muddy body through the opening and into the front seat of the brand new pickup truck. All this happened in some type of weird time warp. I can remember hearing my dad yelling wooh, wooh, wooh at the gun shy champion, and then the complete silence as we stared at this muddy dog sitting in the front seat of Cotton's truck with his tongue hanging out of his mouth. It looked like he was smiling.

A few days later, Cotton dropped by with the bill from Randy's Body Shop and my dad once again appeared to be shucking out bills like he was dealing cards.

I grew up with my pal Dixie the champion. He lived to be 18 years old and never hunted again. Around the holidays when fireworks were going off around the town, we always kept the windows rolled up on our vehicles. Our gun shy champion would always find a hiding place.

THE WEASEL

As I was growing up, my dad owned a bulldozer and a tractor-trailer truck to haul it around. Nothing thrilled me more than to ride in the eighteen-wheeler with him when he hauled his dozer from one job to the next. One hot August day we were taking the dozer to the southern end of the county. As we started up Sheepneck Ridge, which was the steepest hill he had ever tried to pull with his 40 ton Cat D-8 on board, the truck got down to low gear quickly. We were moving slower and slower with no lower gear to go to. The truck was eventually chugging so slow there were smoke rings coming out of the stack. It then bogged down and stopped on what appeared to be the steepest part of the hill. We were in a bind.

My dad locked the air brakes, jumped out of the truck, and grabbed a large wooden block out of the side box of the truck. He threw it behind the tires in order to keep the truck from rolling backwards. The air brakes would not hold forty tons for very long. He was scratching his head wondering what he was going to do next when we heard the deafening sound of some type of engine coming up the hill.

An old B Model Mack came around the bend. Each of the smoke stacks of this Mack was shooting a flame that reached the leaves of the Oak trees that bowed over Sheepneck Ridge Road. For those of you not familiar with the trucking world, a B Model Mack is one of the old timey looking trucks that would be synonymous with a forties model car in the car world. It has a hood that appears to be ten feet long. They were already considered classics at the time of this story and still are.

The driver pulled around us and stopped. If you know anything about trucking, nobody ever stops on a steep hill with a loaded truck for fear of not being able to take off again. Was this guy an idiot? When the driver got out of his truck, we noticed he was only about five feet tall with his boots on. He had more of a waddle than a walk. He only moved his legs about four inches each step he took, but had very quick steps which made him cover a lot of ground. He said his name was Weasel and he asked what our problem was.

My dad told him the load was too heavy to pull up the hill. Weasel said, "Got a chain?" My dad looked at me and then at him with a puzzled look. He then looked at the load of flat steel the driver was already hauling and said, "Yep, I'll get it." My dad knew that there was no way this truck could pull both loads up the hill.

Weasel backed his truck close enough to our truck to hook the chain to our front bumper. He told my dad, "When you see fire coming out of that there stack, give er' all ya got! When you see me change gears, you change gears." Weasel jumped back into his truck and eased his truck forward to tighten the chain.

Weasel had a flatbed trailer with no headboard. We could see him over the flat steel through the back glass of his truck cab. Many of the trucks of that era had what was called a Quadra-Plex transmission. It had two shifting sticks instead of one. They were difficult to drive and you had to reach across the cab to shift the outer stick. To change into certain gears, the driver literally had to put one arm through the steering wheel and shift both sticks at the same time.

We saw the fire shoot out of Weasel's stacks. That was my dad's clue to mash the throttle of his truck. Amazingly Weasel's engine was powerful enough to pull the weight of his load of flat steel and my dad's truck loaded with the bulldozer. Whatever he had for an engine, it didn't come from the factory like that. It had a deafening noise even though we were fifty feet behind and we could feel the ground trembling from the vibration. Weasel stared back at us through the back window with a wild look in his eyes. From time to time, he would take a millisecond glance forward to make sure he was still in his lane.

Each time Weasel changed gears the fire would stop coming out of the smoke stacks as he took his foot off of the throttle. His head would then actually disappear below the rear window as he reached for the gear shifters. He would be gone about two seconds. When the fire shot back out of the stacks, we knew he had mashed his throttle again and had changed gears. About

STEAMBOAT McKENNON

M Y MOTHER WENT to high school with Steamboat McKennon in the late forties. She didn't know his real first name. The teachers also called him Steamboat. She is sure they didn't know his real first name either . . . unless it was Steamboat. My mother claims he was the meanest man she had ever known. He had one weakness. He was petrified of the dark and caught a lot of ribbing from his peers about this flaw. He once knocked a sink off the wall in the high school restroom trying to get out after someone cut the lights off. He gave that person a good beating and nobody ever cut the lights off again in any room that contained Steamboat.

A few years after high school, my mother was eating a late-night supper with some friends at The Rebel Truck Stop on the north end of town. Steamboat was sitting at the pin ball machine minding his own business when the Carroll boys from Hohenwald, a rival town to the west, came in. Fights seemed to follow the Carroll boys and this night would be no exception. It took fifteen minutes or so before one of the Carrolls pushed Billy Joe Roberts down a short flight of stairs. Billy Joe was one of Steamboat's good friends.

My mother watched from under a table as chairs went flying across the room. One of the chairs hit the light in the center of the room which in turn kicked the main breaker making the lights go out. It was pitch dark in The Rebel Truck Stop. She had been around Steamboat enough to recognize his howl as he headed out of the door. He was running from the dark. Since the restaurant was not in the city limits, there were no street lights so it was also dark outside.

Steamboat ran southbound down Highway 43 towards town howling like the Wolfman. The two Carroll boys he had been fighting with mistook Steamboat's flight as being afraid of them rather than the dark. They decided to chase him down. They caught up with him about a quarter mile down the road . . . just about the time he got to the Mount Pleasant city limits which happened to be where the first street light was. Steamboat stopped under the light, wheeled around, and beat up both of them. The Carroll boys later learned why Steamboat was running and realized they had caught a tiger by the tail.

THE CIRCUS COMES TO TOWN

I WORKED WITH A man named Bobby Workman. Bobby and I argued more than any two people on the face of the earth and it wasn't until I was older that I realized he had been correct on most of the points we argued about. Bobby was raised up on Watts Hill south of Mount Pleasant.

Back in the forties the old dirt road that still winds up Watts Hill was the main road between Maury County and Lawrence County. When it rained, cars and trucks would get stuck trying to drive up the hill on the muddy road. Bobby's father made a pretty good living on rainy days pulling these vehicles up the hill with his team of mules.

When Bobby was about ten years old, the circus had been in town and was headed to Lawrence County for their next show. As the circus convoy started up the hill, the caravan of trucks marred up in the mud. To Bobby's dad, it appeared to be a gold mine stuck on the side of the hill. He quickly hooked up his team of mules and headed to the hill side. His dad asked Bobby to stay at the top of the hill and hold on to the mule team while he went halfway down the hill to negotiate with the circus master. Bobby could see the negotiations. The circus master negotiated for a little while, then shook his head in a big no and walked away.

The circus master then said something in a foreign language to the truck drivers and the next thing Bobby knew they were unloading the elephants from the trucks. They hooked these beasts up to the trucks with ropes and these elephants began pulling the trucks up the hill. Bobby was from a poor home and had not been able to go to the circus. Seeing the elephants pull the trucks up Watts Hill was better than being at any circus and left an imprint on his mind that he never forgot.

THE FIRE

WHEN I WAS in my twenties, I went against the wise advice of my father once again and went into the trucking business with a friend of mine. Do you want to know how to end up with five thousand dollars in the bank in the trucking business? Start out with ten thousand dollars in the bank.

One of my drivers became ill in St Louis and had a load on board going to Denver. He called from the hospital and advised me he wasn't going to get out for a few days. I headed to St. Louis in my pickup truck to get the tractor-trailer truck and make sure the load got delivered on time.

I left The Z about 11am headed to St Louis. I happened upon my buddy Pie Face and my younger brother David before I got out of Maury County. I stopped to chat with them and by the end of the conversation the car they were riding in was parked and we were icing down a case of Budweiser getting ready for our trip to Denver via the St Louis hospital.

I will spare you the details of everything in between Columbia and St Louis except for the look on my driver's face when three idiots (one of them his boss) showed up in his hospital room about midnight asking for the keys to the truck. He almost did not relinquish them, which would have been a wise decision. He knew all three of us and knew we were irresponsible to say the least. It took me longer than most to grow up. It runs in the family. Since my brother and I were together, this was a recipe for delinquent behavior. Add Pie Face to the equation, who also had a developmental problem from a maturity standpoint, and it was a wonder we did not get into trouble long before we reached St. Louis.

We arrived in Denver late the next day with very little sleep. The hair on each of our heads was sticking up and we were scary looking. Since we couldn't unload until the next morning, we booked a room in a plush motel on the company credit card and headed to the bar. At midnight, they closed the bar and we headed to the room. The motel was the type that had the room doors opening to an inside hallway that had very plush carpet. There was a fire sprinkler system overhead in the hallway.

When we got to our room, Pie noticed the fire sprinkler on the ceiling just outside our door. In an attempt to be funny he struck a match and held it up to the sprinkler. When the match had burned low enough to burn his finger, he threw it down and struck another one. I told him that he had been watching too much TV and it took several thousand degrees to set those off and would he please come on in the room so we could get some sleep. As I laughed at him and his foolishness, he lit the whole book of matches. I explained to him again how there was no way a book of matches would set the sprinkler off.

Just as I finished the sentence the water pressure knocked us both to our knees. Every sprinkler on our mile long floor was spraying at a hundred and fifty PSI. We jumped up, ran into our room, and slammed the door. Now it was serious. Pie did not think he could set them off either and now that he had succeeded he instantly regretted it. They would never suspect three drunken fools that had walked through the lobby about two and a half minutes earlier that just happened to be staying on that floor.

Have you ever done something dumb, not thinking of all of the consequences? Me too, but this time I was innocent but shared a room with the idiot that did it. Is that guilt by association?

I was standing in the room with water dripping off of my nose wondering how long it would take the motel management to cut off the water when off in the distance I heard it. It was faint and would fade away at first, drowned out by the other noises of the city and far enough away that the breeze had to blow in our direction to carry the sound waves enough to hear it. The sound now grew louder and didn't fade away. I was hearing several sirens. We looked out of our window in time to see ten fire trucks pulling in the parking lot. If I am exaggerating, it is only by a truck or two. This was now serious. We were probably going to jail. I yelled at Pie and my brother to get in bed and not move a muscle. You could have poked me with a pin and I wouldn't have flinched.

The water from the sprinklers had now stopped spraying against the door and we could hear people beating on the doors of our hallway waking people up. They were getting close to our door, but I wasn't going to answer.

About one millisecond before the knock came to our door, a hair dryer fired up. "Noooooooo, Pie . . . you idiot!" Pie was drying his hair. I jumped up and pulled the plug, but the person beating on the door had heard the commotion. I timidly opened the door. Maybe he thought I had just taken a shower . . . It's possible. The large gentleman asked if he could step about three feet into our room and vacuum the water up. I complied.

I did not sleep a wink that night. I thought they would be coming to get us any minute. They never did. Maybe the guy at the door realized we were just a trio of dumb country boys that should have known better. I will never know why we didn't get arrested. We certainly deserved to spend at least that night in jail. I never went back to Denver. I always feared my face was on a wanted poster out there. I also never took another road trip with Pie Face or my brother. We are all three grown up and gray-headed now, but even today if the three of us got together we would probably revert to a state of immaturity . . . but that will never happen.

The Games People Play

ORKING IN A large plant like Victor Chemical can become monotonous. In a perfect setting the plant management would have assigned one supervisor to each worker so nobody would go astray, but the bottom line of a company can rarely afford such a luxury. With one supervisor watching over ten workers, it is possible for a worker or two to go astray. If I had been a supervisor at Victor Chemical, I am sure I would not have been able to keep my eye on all ten of my underlings. I am also sure that, just as a defensive back is told by the coach to follow one particular opposing all-star, I would have definitely kept my eye on Tooterbill at all times.

Since this was a chemical plant, the workers were not allowed to wear their street clothes past the locker room and were not allowed to go home in their work clothes. Workers reported to work and changed into white company-provided coveralls. At the end of their shift, they removed the coveralls, put them into a mesh cotton bag with their name embroidered on the tag, and chunked them into a large motel-like rolling container to be washed. Each worker was assigned two sets of coveralls which were washed after each alternating shift. Tooterbill had been reassigned to the wash room after the 'accident' on July 4th. That seemed the logical place for a middle-aged man that had been deemed to have a slight lack of maturity.

Every facility in the country that works over fifty or so people has at least one of those guys that seems to get the brunt of practical jokes. Just think back to high school. It was the same way. There are usually a couple of people that get picked on more than the general population. In the case of Victor, Seth Hodge was the one. He was a very likable guy, but was very gullible. Everyone liked him, but everyone also liked to pick on him.

Each time Seth turned his coveralls in to be washed, Tooterbill would use a company sewing machine to take the hemline of Seth's coverall pants legs up a sixteenth of an inch. He didn't want to decrease the hemline too much or Seth may have noticed. As most practical jokers do, Tooterbill alerted all of the hourly workers to his scheme who in turn would check out the daily progress of Seth's coveralls slowly turning into high-water britches.

As weeks went by, Seth's pants legs began approaching the top of his socks. He just assumed his pants were shrinking and figured he would hold out until they switched the coveralls out for new ones which happened every three months or so. It wasn't until you could see the skin of his legs between the bottom of his pants leg and his socks that Seth went to the wash room supervisor to complain about the poor quality of his coveralls. Since nobody else in the plant had this shrinking problem, it didn't take long for the supervisor to figure out what the cause of the quality problem was.

Tooterbill once again sat in the HR manager's office denying he had anything to do with this hostile act. Since it could not be proven that he had violated any specific company policies, he was sent back to work with a stern finger pointing. Seth was issued new coveralls and was told to come to the supervisor at the first sign of shrinkage.

THE HYBRID TRUCK

$\mathcal{S}$ETH HAD RECENTLY purchased a small economy-size pickup truck. He was bragging in the lunch room about how it was getting twenty-five miles per gallon which was five miles per gallon higher than the manufacturers estimated MPG on the sticker. Tooterbill heard this conversation and began to devise his next prank. Each day, Tooterbill would stop by Wimp's Market on the way to work and fill a plastic container with a gallon of gas. At lunch each day he would sneak into the parking lot and put this gas into Seth's pickup truck. He would let him get low enough to actually have to purchase gas every few weeks. It was a carefully controlled prank.

Seth suddenly quit bragging about his gas mileage and seemed to avoid the subject when Tooterbill would ask him what kind of mileage he was getting. After a few weeks, Seth confided in a friend and told him he was getting three hundred miles per gallon. He swore his friend to secrecy for fear people would think he was crazy if he told them. He feared he would be ostracized like people who claim they have been abducted by aliens. His friend, who already knew of the prank, went to Tooterbill and told him enough was enough.

Tooterbill agreed to back off but wasn't finished just yet. In Tooterbill's mind, Seth owed him some gas, so he would now sneak out at lunch each day and use a piece of garden hose to siphon about a gallon of gas out of Seth's truck. Seth went from three hundred miles per gallon to ten miles per gallon in a week.

The service manager at Lucas Chevrolet went through the motions for Seth after hearing of what was going on with his new truck. He was sure Seth was crazy, but the customer is king. They couldn't find any problems with his fuel system and after word got out that he had taken the truck back to the dealer for the ten miles per gallon problem, the friend once again threatened

Tooterbill with exposure. The fuel problems went away and Seth went back to getting twenty-five miles per gallon like he did when he first purchased the truck. He never mentioned his gas mileage again.

THE MARKSMAN

I WENT TO HIGH school at Columbia Military Academy in Columbia, Tennessee. This was a classic military school with huge WWI era stone buildings that were once used to house soldiers. Once a week we had 'rifle range' class on the top floor of the old armory building. We were issued single shot 22 caliper rifles and ten rounds of ammunition. We fired at targets taped to hay bails. It was well controlled by the military personnel that were assigned to the school. When the shooting was over, you had better have ten empty shell cartridges to turn in or you were in serious trouble. They did not want students going back to class with live ammo, so they verified we had fired all of our bullets. A missing shell casing resulted in an uncomfortable search for the entire class.

One of the people in this class was an expert marksman and proud of it. William was actually an Olympic hopeful and almost made the cut a few years after graduation. If you know anything about marksmanship, a good shooter will have a very tight pattern of holes which means he or she is very accurate. For instance, after I fired at my target 10 times, holes would be scattered all over the target which means I was not accurate. It may not necessarily have 10 holes since I could easily miss a 12 by 12 inch target by several inches when firing from seventy-five feet away.

William on the other hand would have a perfect pattern that was so tight it would resemble one large hole right in the bulls eye as if he had shot a mini-ball at the target. There was no doubt this guy was good. This is what the instructor wanted to see . . . no stray bullet holes on the target and a very tight pattern. Since he was the best in the class and I was the worst, he would make it a point to compare targets with me.

It occurred to me one day that since he was so good, there was no way anyone could count the number of times he hit the target since his tight pattern merely created one large hole in the middle. Everyone always correctly assumed he had put all ten rounds in the center to decimate the paper target and create one large hole. On the other hand, I was so bad that if I only had nine individual holes in my target, the instructor would easily assume I had missed as long as I produced ten empty cartridges. About once a month, by chance, William would end up in the space next to me as we fired away on the rifle range.

I only had to move the barrel of my rifle an unnoticeable two inches to the right to be able to zero in on his target instead of mine. On this shot, I would take special care to follow all the shooting procedures because I wanted to make sure that I hit his target in just the right spot which was about five inches below the bull's eye and his tight pattern. On one unlucky day per month, he would have one big glob of perfect shots directly in the bulls eye and one bullet hole that looked like he pulled the trigger with his eyes closed. If I had put as much effort into hitting my own target with a perfect shot as I did with his, I would have made the Olympics.

At the end of these sessions, I would turn in my target, turn in my weapon and my ten empty cartridges, and walk out of the door while William swore up and down to the instructor that the stray hole could not possibly be his or else his rifle was malfunctioning. He was too good and he knew it. I would fight the smile until I was out of the armory so I would not become a suspect. Until now, he never knew it was me.

THE PAINTER

A T COLUMBIA MILITARY Academy we were required to line up each morning before class for inspection. If our shoes and belt buckles were not shined, we received demerits. After receiving five demerits in a month, you had to walk what was called 'the bullring". The bullring was a square asphalt road about the size of half a football field. Each demerit equaled one hour walking this square with a fifty pound pack on your back and a non-functioning rifle handed down by the military from wars gone by in your hands.

Every class has a class clown. Ours was Edwin Raspberry. He was not only the class clown, but the school clown. All classes and grades knew of his exploits. Edwin showed up one morning and had failed to shine his shoes. Using a figure of speech that I am sure came from a Gomer Pyle episode, the platoon leader yelled at Edwin, "In the morning those shoes had better be painted boy. Do you understand me boy? I want them painted!" Edwin acknowledged that he clearly understood.

The next morning Edwin arrived and had painted his shoes purple with a paintbrush. He kept a straight face and swore he thought that is what the platoon leader had meant. Each day for the next couple of months as we left to go home, we would wave goodbye to Edwin as he walked around the bullring with his backpack, his hand-me-down rifle, and his goofy smile.

THEY WEREN'T PAYING ATTENTION

WHEN I WAS in the tenth grade a police officer come to our school to give us a speech on drug abuse. It was a military school and it was 1972, so there were many people at school that were already well educated on drug abuse. The officer, who told us this was his first visit to a military academy, wanted to show us what a marijuana cigarette looked like. He passed a fake joint around on a small tray so everyone could see it up close and know what not to smoke.

I was in the eighth row and by the time it passed by me, it already had his fake joint plus two other real joints on the tray. When it got back up front, the tray had six joints on it. Some of the geniuses I was going to school with had not been paying attention. They thought when the tray passed by, he was giving them an opportunity to come clean before the search.

The surprised officer put the joints in a plastic evidence bag, dismissed us, and headed to the commandant's office. We never saw him or anyone else on a similar mission again.

THE BARRISTERS DREAM
(OR NIGHTMARE)

HEARD A STORY just after the L.A. riots about two young men that were on trial for looting an electronics store. The prosecuting attorney had a witness on the stand and asked, "Did you get a good look at the two men that took the television sets from the store?"

The witness replied, "Yes, I did."

The prosecuting attorney then asked, "Are the two men that took the television sets in this courtroom?"

Before the witness had a chance to reply, the two defendants that were on trial for taking the televisions raised their hands. They thought the prosecutor was asking them to identify themselves.

Their frantic defense attorney attempted to slam their hands down, but the damage was done.

On a more local note, Jerry Lee Brown ran a little county store on the south end of Mount Pleasant about a mile from the starting point of The Z. It was rumored you could get about anything you wanted there and all of it wasn't on the shelves. Selling pills usually required you to graduate from pharmacy school. Jerry Lee didn't even finish high school but sold more pills than the pharmacy on the town square. I stopped in there every now and then at lunch time because he also made a mean bologna and cheese sandwich.

Jerry Lee had been arrested a few weeks earlier for growing marijuana on his farm. The key piece of evidence against him was four hundred feet of garden hose running from the water faucet on the side of his house to the garden sprinkler in the middle of the patch. The fact his fingerprints were found on the sprinkler didn't help his case. Open and shut, right? Well, that's what most people thought.

I was out there one day eating a bologna and cheese sandwich. I said, "Jerry Lee, I hope you get out of that mess you're in."

Jerry Lee told me, "Let me tell you where most people make their mistake son. They go out and get a high-priced lawyer and blow all their money. I went out and got a cheap lawyer and am paying my witnesses well!" He never cracked a smile when he said it.

Jerry Lee was acquitted and never served a day.

THE MOON

A GREAT FRIEND OF mine is named Moon. He got the name one Saturday night when he mooned a bunch of people that were tailgating at the Gulf station on Main Street. I was in the car along with several other hard-ankles (guys) when this happened. Moon was a little overweight, so his rear end took up every cubic inch of the rear window of the '57 Chevy we were riding in. His rear end molded into a shape that matched the shape of the window.

The Mount Pleasant police just happened to be parked on the other side of the station. I remember the spotlight hitting his rump like it was yesterday. It actually shined like the moon. Needless to say he was ticketed for some technical law book term that meant 'mooning' and hence got a nickname that has stuck with him to this day. I guess us passengers were accessories to a mooning, but no charges were filed against us. He was put on eleven months and twenty nine days probation and assigned a probation officer.

A few months later, my sister invited me to meet her and her husband at their cabin on the Duck River. She told me to bring a friend or two. We loaded up as many people as would fit into Moon's fifty-eight Oldsmobile, iced down a case of Budweiser Tall Boys, and headed to the river. We were all under age, but if a three year old had the money, he or she could buy beer at Jerry Lee's on the south side of town. You could also buy cigarettes or valium with food stamps for fifty cents on the dollar. It was a classy joint.

When we arrived at the cabin, we all got a fresh Budweiser in our hand so we would look cool to my older sister and brother-in-law. We walked in and each of us simultaneously chugged a big sip in stride to show what underage men we were. Moon choked on his and spewed it all over my sister, her husband, and their guest. Sitting at the table in a remote cabin at least thirty miles from civilization was Moon's probation officer. Moon was busted.

Did I mention that my brother-in-law was also a probation officer? Moon knew my sister and brother-in-law well, but who would have thought they would bring a friend that happened to be Moon's probation officer. My sister knew their friend was a probation officer, but had no idea Moon was his client. Moon and his surprise cabin mate went out on the porch for a while and had a discussion.

We had a ball that weekend and caught a lot of fish. We woke up each morning feeling great because the strongest thing we had the rest of the weekend was iced tea.

THE PAINTING CREW

I HAD A SHORT term loss of judgment a decade or so ago and took a transfer to Ft Wayne, Indiana. There are great people up there and it is a great area, so the following statement is regarding the weather only. If I had a brother in prison and a brother in northern Indiana, I would try to get the one in Indiana out first. The northern Indiana winters just about killed this ole Tennessee boy! I have no idea how it ever got populated up there.

One of my first projects after arriving was to paint the house I had just purchased. Being a poor boy from Tennessee, I could not afford to hire anyone to paint it for me. It was a two story wood-sided house with a very tall chimney slightly shorter than the Empire State Building. The roof had a pitch almost as steep as a cliff.

I had plenty of rope since I had just moved. When hillbillies move, they use plenty of rope and have things sticking out of windows. My grown son Marc and I climbed carefully onto the roof. He was on one side of the roof peak and I was on the other. We then took a ten foot piece of rope and tied it around each of our waists. This is starting to sound like a 'hey ya'll, watch this'.

Well, you got it. In order to paint the chimney I would tell him, "Ok, move up 3 feet". That of course would move me down three feet on the other side of the roof. We continued this maneuver, inching our way up and down the roof the length of the chimney until we had accomplished the paint job. Our new neighbors, whom my wife had looked forward to meeting and making a good impression on, were riding by gawking and must have been thinking, "That must be the way those idiots do it in the south". Well, I let them keep believing that even though I had never seen this done in Tennessee either.

With the money we saved doing it ourselves, we were able to afford the co-pay at the doctor's office and crutch rental when I slid off the roof and landed in the driveway. We untied the rope slightly earlier than we should have.

THE ICE FISHERMAN

WHILE LIVING IN the frozen tundra of Indiana, I would pass by a small lake each morning as I left for work. During the wintertime (which was about ten months of the year up there) several people would be sitting out on the iced-over lake with fishing poles in their hands. I would often wonder why I had to work for a living while these people got to go fishing every day. Then it dawned on me . . . they can't work because they would never be able to pass a pre-employment drug screen. They even had fires built on the ice. Wouldn't you think the fire would melt the ice and they would just fall through?

Seeing these demented northerners fish each frigid morning always reminded me of a time when my younger brother David decided to become an ice fisherman while growing up in Tennessee. I was about 12, so he would have been 10. Although the Tennessee winters do not compare to the Indiana winters, it does get cold enough to freeze a pond every so often. The difference in Tennessee and Indiana is when it gets cold in Tennessee there is still hope of warm days in the near future. It gets cold, then warm, then cold, warm . . . etc . . . In Indiana, once it gets cold, your only hope for a warm day is April.

This particular winter we were in a long cold spell. It was one of those rare times in the south that the ponds froze over solid enough to walk on without the danger of breaking through the ice. We had a pond about a half a mile behind our house about the size of a three car garage that probably didn't even have minnows, much less fish.

With my mama's daily speech of, "If you get on that pond you're going to get a whipping" fresh on his mind, my brother snuck his fishing pole and our daddy's hatchet out of the basement and headed to the pond. He chopped a two foot diameter hole in the middle of the pond, put a frozen worm on his hook, and proceeded to fish. He was a shade of light blue when he returned home with no fish. He secretly told me of his fishing trip in a whisper so mama wouldn't hear and how several large fish had pulled the float under and almost pulled him through the hole, but he just couldn't bring one in. I thought nothing more of his tall tale and went to bed.

The next morning, my buddy Sammy Boshers knocked on the door as he did most Saturday mornings. He wanted to go on a hike. I dressed in my winter clothes and headed out with Sammy and my brother. It had snowed about 2 inches overnight and we were sure we could track some wild animals in the fresh snow. We headed back through the woods, and inevitably came to . . . the pond.

We knew better than to walk on it, but we were out of sight of all adults and it looked like fun. My brother's previous day fishing trip never entered my mind. He was with us and it didn't cross his mind either. The problem was that most of the pond was frozen about six inches thick, but there was a two foot diameter hole in the middle that had only had time to re-freeze about an inch thick overnight.

The fresh snow on the pond looked like a carpet with no hint of the hole created the previous day. Twelve and ten year old boys can remember batting averages and the price of candy at the dime store, but the ice fishing expedition from the previous day had been purged from the minds of both of us . . . and Sammy didn't have a clue about the expedition of the previous day.

I had seen people fall through ice on television before, but they don't get it right. They show a slow fall with a splash and arms flailing. Sammy simply disappeared. One second we were walking, the next he was gone and there was a hole in the ice between my brother and me. It was at that point we both thought, "Oh yea, David chopped a hole in the ice yesterday." Exactly one trillionth of a second later, Sammy sprang up out of the three foot deep water and was standing beside us again. It wasn't even over his head, but with the surprise he didn't have time to catch himself with his legs. He went under.

I have about a hundred seconds worth of memories of this, but all of what I just told you took less than a second. You would have to study Einstein's relativity theory to make any sense of that, but if my brother and I had simultaneously blinked, it would have been as if Sammy was dry one second and no hole existed in the pond, then wet standing beside a hole in the pond a second later. We would not have known he had gone in and back out. The weird thing was he had the same expression on his face afterwards as before. It happened so fast he didn't even have time to change expressions.

Have you ever had one of those moments with a group of people that you all had the exact same thought at the same time? Well this was one of those times. We didn't think "Wow, that was close, Sammy could have drowned!" or "Boy, we were dumb to not remember that hole was there." Our simultaneous thought was, "We're all gonna get a 'whippin'!"

It was blue cold that morning. After walking about two hundred yards back towards our houses we realized that Sammy's blue jeans had frozen stiff. He was walking like he was on stilts. His jeans actually looked like something that had been in the freezer and had freezer burn. Our house was about a quarter mile closer than Sammy's house, so that would have been the logical place to go for warmth. The problem was that if my mother saw his frozen jeans, she would know that we had been on that pond. We could lie and say that Sammy went on the pond by himself, but we knew she would whip us for letting him get on the pond. He was one of my best friends, but I had to stand my ground, "You ain't going to my house."

We hid in the fence row behind my house for a while negotiating this dilemma. Sammy had figured out he could go to my house, borrow some of my clothes, and escape the sure whippin' at his house. After all, my blue jeans and gray sweatshirt looked just like his blue jeans and gray sweatshirt. Only David and I would get a spanking in this scenario. That would work out better for Sammy.

Since there were two of us and one of him, he lost the battle of the wills and headed home having to actually swing his legs outward in a wide arc as he walked to keep his feet from dragging the ground due to his frozen jeans. My brother and I went straight to our rooms at about 25 miles per hour. This was a dead giveaway in itself on a Saturday morning. We thought our mother would think nothing of it and ask no questions.

We both held up well during the intense questioning from dear mom. She would not have gotten it out of us if she had tortured us by swinging a banana in front of our eyes with a bright light in the background, but Sammy had to cave to his mother. There was just no way to explain frozen blue jeans.

We all got our deserved whipping that morning. Sammy got his one and only whipping of the day for going on the pond. David and I got our first one for going on the pond, our second one for lying about it, and the third one for not letting Sammy come inside our house to warm up and put on dry clothes. I got a fourth one for letting my younger brother go on the pond. The trouble with four whippings is you don't know when one whipping has ended and another has begun. To me it was just one loooonnngg whipping.

If only Sammy's mother had kept quiet and not called my mother, only Sammy would have gotten his just reward for not listening to adults!

THE WRENCH

I GREW UP ON Fairview Drive at the end of The Z. It intersects Washington Avenue near the top of Rippey's Hill. The top quarter mile of Washington Avenue is as steep as hills come. It doglegs to the right at the bottom of the steep part and then gently slopes downhill for another half mile or so. The founding fathers of our city, in their infinite wisdom, put a fire hydrant at the top of the hill.

At some point through the years, one of the neighborhood kids had illegally obtained a fire hydrant wrench on the black market. It was kept in a clump of bushes in the Brown's yard at the corner of Washington and Fairview and everyone on that leg of The Z under twenty-one knew where it was located. It was the best kept secret in town and not one parent or city official knew it existed. You could 'rat out' someone for throwing water balloons at cars or for setting off firecrackers in the Jackson's garage, but the information teams at Guantanamo Bay would not have succeeded in getting knowledge of the existence of this wrench from any of us . . . it didn't exist.

Washington Avenue was the place that all the kids gathered to go sledding when our once a year snowstorm struck. All of the adults knew the protocol of blowing the car horn when attempting to get up the hill after a snowstorm since so many kids were present. This was before the days of every other family owning a four wheel drive vehicle. If you heard a horn blowing continuously off in the distance, roll off of your sled and get out of the road because a fast moving vehicle was gaining steam on the long straight stretch of Washington Avenue in an attempt to make it up the last steep quarter mile.

All adults that lived on 'The Hill' also knew another protocol. If you needed supplies to last out the few days before the thaw, you had better go to town on the first day of the snowstorm because after nightfall came, there was no getting your automobile back up the hill no matter how much velocity you obtained on the straight stretch. Once the sun went down two things were certain: The temperature would plummet enough for water to quickly freeze and someone under twenty-one would get 'the wrench'. We would open the fire hydrant at the top of the hill for about thirty minutes and watch as the water gushed out and soaked the packed snow of Washington Avenue.

Not only had the founding fathers had the forethought to put a hydrant at the top of the hill, but whoever installed it had actually pointed the nozzle at a perfect angle towards the street. Within a couple of hours of opening the hydrant, a person could only cross Washington on their hands and knees. It became as slick as glass.

If someone went to town after that and was fortunate enough to get down the hill without sliding into the ditch, they had to park at the Grissom's house at the bottom of the hill on the return trip and walk the last quarter mile. Every now and then a daring neighbor would attempt to go all the way to the top after 'the icing', but their car would go straight into the Ross's yard at the dogleg and remain there like a warning beacon for anyone else that thought about an attempt.

The main reason for icing the street was to be able to sled down the hill as fast as possible. You have seen the cartoons where the character takes off so fast that their hat stays behind. The top of Washington Avenue was soon littered with hats after the water froze. Once you got on your sled, you had better be ready to go, because it would take off as if it had an engine on it!

You could sled all the way to town if you remembered to drag your toes at the dogleg to slow down enough to make the curve. If you didn't remember, you ended up in the Ross's yard with the cars of neighbors that didn't get their supplies before the first night and had attempted to make it back to the top.

Next time I make my way back to town, I may check out the bushes in the Brown's yard just to see if the wrench is still there. If it happens to be the night after a snowstorm, I may become the first adult in town history to open the hydrant.

THE BLIZZARD

A FEW YEARS AFTER my brother's ice fishing incident, we had a blizzard in our town. Yes, a blizzard in Tennessee. Well, it was cold and it did snow about eight inches and they did close the grocery store, hence, a blizzard. It was my senior year in high school. I was seventeen and my brother was fifteen.

Parents, always beware of who your kids are hanging out with. Ninety percent of what they do will be influenced by their peers. The problem was that David was hanging out with me. My mother was very careful about the people we hung out with, but the fact that my brother should not hang out with me had never crossed her mind. For that matter, it had never crossed her mind that I shouldn't be hanging out with my older sisters. Mary Anna, my oldest sister, was the neighborhood co-gang leader along with Bill Ross and my sister Leslie was their first lieutenant. Now . . . this wasn't a gang like you would see in the Bronx, but we still felt like a gang.

Each year Jack Lonefoot, a neighborhood parent and Oklahoma native, would go to Tulsa for a family reunion. We looked forward to his return because he would always bring back approximately twenty cases of Coors beer. In the mid 70's Coors could only be purchased west of the Mississippi River which made it a delicacy on this side of the river. Borrowing just enough Coors out of his basement so he wouldn't miss it had become a tradition each year after he returned.

People who buy beer in twenty case allotments and drink a good bit never miss a case or two. They assume they drank it themselves. It was about this time that I found out that the older kids had been stealing my dad's Falstaff out of our basement for years. He bought it in large quantities about once a month. I think back and wonder why my parents simply didn't lock the basement door that led to the outside? Why didn't Jack lock his outside door to the basement? We never committed breaking and entering, just entering and taking. My brother and I kept our mouth shut about the pilfering of our family fortune. We would have had to rat out my two older sisters if we told our parents. They were both regular Falstaff drinkers.

One particular night during this Tennessee blizzard we had built a fire at the top of Washington Avenue and were sipping on Coors and Falstaff. We would take an occasional sled down the hill. We had never allowed my younger brother or the other younger kids to drink before this night. The reason we didn't normally let the younger kids have beer was not because we were worried about their welfare. Underage drinkers do not have a moral objection to letting even younger underage drinkers have alcohol. We weren't old enough to have even pondered that. It was because we did not usually have enough beer to go around. Well, this particular night we had hit the Lonefoot's and the McGaw's pretty hard, so we had enough to stock a shelf at Neeley's Liquor Store.

I can remember the first beer I ever drank. It tasted like dirt. It had taken me a year or two to acquire the taste. Looking back on this night, my brother evidently acquired the taste in about fifteen minutes. As we all talked the next day, nobody really remembered how much he had consumed. He certainly couldn't help us with the math.

The fact we were discussing it the next day should tell you that my brother had gone down in neighborhood history. This event, though long held a secret among kids, eventually got passed on to the adults once we became adults and the 'kid's code of silence' no longer applied to anything except 'the wrench' which is still a closely guarded secret to this day.

I didn't see him get up from his seat by the fire. All I heard was a yaaahhoooo as he went by. He had pulled his sled high up into the woods above Washington Avenue. This gave him about a twenty-five yard running start before actually starting the normal sledding track. When the skids of his sled hit the solid sheet of ice on Washington Avenue he already had considerable momentum. The fact that I was on Coors number five probably influenced my eyesight, but he was a blur as he went by. His coat was lying by the fire. It was like an old western where the actor leaves his possessions behind because he knows he will never return.

We all jumped up, craned our necks, and simultaneously leaned as he went around the dogleg at the bottom of the steep part of the hill. Our leaning was similar to what people do when they attempt a long putt as if it will make the ball go one way or the other by body motion. We were trying to make him miss the curb and the oak trees. We had never seen anybody go down this fast since Bill Ross did it on a skateboard. I guess I should tell you about that in the next chapter.

Somehow my brother made it. We watched him go off into the distance forever brazened in our minds. Although he would be remembered forever in neighborhood history, he was soon forgotten about for the night as we went back to the fire and our stolen alcohol. The fact that he was my brother did make the thought cross my mind as I got up a few hours later to go home, "I haven't seen David in a while."

As much as I didn't want to go down the hill again, I got on my sled and headed down Washington to see if I could find him. One of my buddies was kind enough to ride double with me to help me look.

We found him face down in the snow near the end of Washington Avenue. He was still holding the pull rope of his sled in one hand and a Coors in the other. His body was pointed back up the hill as if he had ended his ride and had started pulling his sled on the return trip. He had apparently passed out in mid-stride. The warmth of his face had caused the packed snow to melt in the shape of his face so that his face was buried two inches deep in the snow.

When we rolled him over, there was a perfect mold of his face in the packed snow. You could see the lips curled up in a smile in the molded snow. We put him on the sled and pulled him to my buddy's house. He fortunately lived at the bottom of the steep part of the hill. We took my brother's wet clothes off and could not believe our eyes. Have you ever seen the Smurf cartoon? He was blue.

When I think back on this situation, we were foolish for not taking him to the emergency room. We covered him up and periodically checked to make sure he was getting some color back. I called my mother and informed her that we were both spending the night with our friend. She asked a few suspicious questions, but let me off the hook.

The next morning, my brother had a 'stomach virus' and short-term memory loss. My unsuspecting mother took care of him as any mother takes care of a sick child. I am sure my brother would have frozen to death if I had not gone looking for him. I am not going to use this to preach against alcohol, but I am aware of how many tragedies start out as a good time. This is an experience we can fortunately look back on and laugh about when we all gather every five years or so at Wophead Ted's house for his annual Christmas open house.

I have not had a drink in twenty years or so. My brother, who still takes a nip now and then, refuses to drink when it snows.

A Hero Remembered

Every town has one or two hometown heroes that are known well outside the boundaries of the city limits. One such hero from our town was Bill Ross. He attended a private school about thirty miles north of Mount Pleasant called Battle Ground Academy. He became a football star and signed a full ride scholarship with Vanderbilt after his senior season which tells you he had the brains to go with the speed.

Bill grew up in our neighborhood and we all knew he was a hero long before his football exploits. He wasn't afraid of anything and would always go that extra step that all of us were afraid to take. The day he is best remembered for was a hot summer day around 1967 or so. I was about ten or eleven, so Bill would have been fourteen or fifteen. Washington Avenue was as steep as any hill in the county with a heck of a dogleg at the bottom. Many people had made it around the dogleg on sleds, but nobody had ever made the turn on a skateboard. Skateboards had just come on the scene in recent years and Bill had a cool one with a Shark painted on it. The skateboards of the day were crude and basically consisted of roller skates screwed onto a painted piece of plywood.

Bill announced to us that he was going to give Washington a try. We all gathered at the dogleg to see the accident. Bill tucked his skateboard under his arm and headed the quarter mile towards the top of the hill.

Once he got to the very top, he stood and stared down the hill for several minutes like a downhill skier does before leaving the gate. We saw him mount and give a push off with his right leg and lean forward. He looked like he was doing 60 mph as he came down the hill. As he got closer to us, the skateboard wheels sounded like a jet engine as they rolled on the pavement. He appeared to be leaning forward at such an angle that his face was only two feet off of the pavement. I don't know what his actual speed was, but he was going faster than we had ever seen a sled go down the hill, even after it had become a sheet of ice due to opening the fire hydrant. There was no way he could make the turn.

When he got to the dogleg, he had to lean hard to the right to make his skateboard turn. It appeared as if his right shoulder would touch the ground. We were all gathered on the side of the street that he was leaning towards. Just when it looked like he was a goner and as he was leaning the most, he cut his eyes over at us, lifted a Pepsi Cola to his lips with his right arm, and took a big drink. He was completely under control and unafraid. He then straightened out and headed towards town and into neighborhood history.

Bill was killed in a car wreck near Franklin Tennessee the summer after he graduated from High School. He never made it to Vanderbilt. Our town and the world lost a hero.

The Nine Hundred Dollar Boat

M Y DAD HAD an old wooden fishing boat that had made a thousand or so trips around the banks of Arrow Lake on the south end of Mount Pleasant. It had been about a year since he had been fishing, so he decided to sell his boat. A couple of years earlier, the boat had sprung a leak and he had patched it with black tar. It wasn't pretty, but it sealed the leak. The boat motor was like a brand new one and was probably worth a thousand bucks by itself without the boat.

He put a classified add in The Daily Herald that read 'Fishing boat and motor $900'. He then mounted the motor on a fifty-five gallon barrel filled with water so he could crank the engine when people came to look at the boat. This kept water flowing through the engine keeping it cool so it wouldn't damage it while testing. People would hear the motor running perfectly and would be grinning and ready to buy it until they saw the black patch on the boat. My dad heard "thank you very much" more than Elvis' tour manager as the potential boat buyers would leave never to return after seeing the black patch on his boat.

After the tenth or so person left without buying the boat, he decided to change his marketing strategy. I have mentioned before that my dad was very smart. He called the Herald and changed it to, 'Boat motor $900. Free boat if you buy the motor'. He sold it thirty minutes after the paper hit the stands. Nobody cared if their free boat had been patched with black tar.

THE FISHERMEN

M Y YOUNGEST SON and I got up one Saturday morning and decided to go fishing. We loaded our poles into my pickup truck and headed to Arrow Lake. We stopped by Stretch Pruitt's store on the way and bought a box of worms. When we arrived at the lake we rented a small flat bottom boat and rowed over to the far side of the lake. The shallow water on the far side was covered with Lilly Pads. I figured the fish would probably like to hide under these large green pads that floated on the water.

We each had on some type of silly hat like experienced fishermen wear, so we looked like we knew what we were doing. We each put a worm on our hook and started fishing. As soon as my line hit the water, a fish pulled my float under. The same thing happened to Jacob's float. We had found the fish. The problem was when we snatched the pole to catch the fish, the fish let go of the hook. When we would pull the line in, the worm would be gone. They would hit the line immediately each time it hit the water and steal our worms. These were either some brilliant fish or we had a problem with our hooks.

I changed each of our hooks to a larger hook. It had no effect. I tried smaller hooks, but still had no luck. I then got creative about how to put the worm on the hook. This didn't work either. It was now a battle of wills. I was going to catch one of these fish if it was the last thing I did. I taped two hooks together trying to trick the fish into thinking there was only one hook hoping I would snag one of them in the side since they apparently weren't going to actually bite the hook. I guess the fish figured that one out too.

We would have stayed out hours more, but the sun was going down in the west. The fish had won. We rowed back across the lake to the boathouse. "How'd ya do?" asked Mr. Mangrum who managed the lake. I replied, "We didn't do too well. We got at least a hundred bites, but we simply could not reel one in."

95

"Ah, you must have been over yonder in those Lilly Pads. The fish over there are so small they can't open their mouths wide enough to get the hook inside. They just suck the worm right off of the hook."

I looked at him out of the corner of my eyes for a couple of seconds, and then paid him the ten bucks for the boat rental. I couldn't help but think that he could have told us about this when he heard us talking about going to the other side of the lake when we first rented the boat. I guess he figured he was ten dollars richer and hadn't lost any fish.

Jacob and I didn't have any fish to eat, but we sure had a ball fighting the little worm sucking creatures for the entire afternoon. It was sure more fun than sitting there all day without getting a bite. We stopped at Stretch's store on the way back through town, picked up a couple of bologna sandwiches, and headed home.

THE SNAKE

BILLY OSBORNE COULD not read or write. He had a way of telling things like no other person on earth. Billy's wife was terrified of snakes. It didn't matter if it was a rattler or a garden snake, she would scream and literally run through the closed screen door. They had no glass doors at their house. She pulled a few splinters from her head now and then and Billy had gotten pretty good at replacing hinges.

Until now all snakes the family had encountered were outside the house. This particular night they came home from Sunday night church and proceeded to enter the house as usual. Billy saw it just as Alice went by the living room closet. A large, harmless black snake had somehow gotten into the house and had slithered through the jackets to the top of the closet and had its neck (does a snake have a neck?) protruding about a foot into the room over the top of the partially-open closet door. Billy said its tongue looked like a frog tongue it stuck out so far. His wife was busy talking and picking up things around the closet as this anaconda, which she had not seen, was about six inches above her head attempting to lick her ear.

Billy knew if she saw the snake, they were moving that night. Best case scenario was that he would have to empty all closets and pull the covers off of all beds every night for the rest of his life.

The cool and calm Billy walked past her and the snake as if nothing was wrong, picked up the Sunday paper from the coffee table, and eased into his favorite chair as he always did. He couldn't read, so I always wondered why this was his normal routine, but that is what he told me. I guess he looked at the pictures. The snake's tongue was now coming within micro millimeters of his wife's ear every time it stuck out. With nerves of steel, Billy was checking out the funnies as his unsuspecting wife told him about some incident earlier in the day. Her story took an eternity and he didn't hear a thing she said.

97

She finally went into the restroom and closed the door. With the speed of a jaguar, Billy grabbed a broom and swatted the snake down to the floor. Fortunately for him, it coiled up which allowed him to open the kitchen door leading to the outside and chip the snake out as if he was going for a par on hole number 18. To my knowledge, Billy had never played golf, but it worked. The toilet flushed and his wife came back out of the restroom. Billy was in the chair looking at pictures in his Sunday paper as if he had never moved. His wife never knew what happened until now. She can read and they may be moving!

DOG'S BEST FRIEND

I WORKED CONSTRUCTION WITH a man named Harvey Isabell. He was in his sixties when I was in my early twenties. Harvey had been hit in the head by a truck rim while changing a flat about ten years earlier and had developed a condition which made him fall asleep at odd times. One of the places that this condition seemed to occur on a regular basis was during lunch break when Harvey's pace had slowed down a bit.

We ate lunch under a large oak tree each day. We gathered around in a circle and sat on bales of straw, sacks of concrete, or upside down buckets. We had a dog that lived at the construction site. Each day during lunch the dog would sit in front of Harvey with his head cocked slightly to the side and wait. Harvey ate a sandwich every day. Every third day or so he would fall asleep while eating.

Harvey could balance on a five gallon bucket while asleep. He would sway a little, but his body would compensate. His hand would drop as if he were handing the sandwich to the dog. The dog would jump forward, grab the sandwich, and chomp it down. Harvey would come to, curse the dog, and go get a pack of crackers out of the vending machine. It became a ritual for the rest of us to watch. We would place bets on whether Harvey or the dog would eat the sandwich each day while Harvey cursed us for talking about it.

I often wondered why Harvey didn't pick a better place to eat. I think back now and wonder if it was as fun for him as it was for us . . . and the dog.

THE CELEBRATION

ALLOWEEN IS A big event in my hometown. As a kid, I could not wait to dress up like Marshal Dillon or the Wolfman and go shake down my neighbors for some treats. When I became a teenager, I would head to Butch's Market which was just off of The Z. That is the place all the delinquents gathered to throw eggs at cars. If you planned to carry your kids trick-or-treating, it was imperative to get back home before dark or you would more than likely be washing your car when you got home.

The best time I ever had on Halloween was when I was in my late twenties and too old to be going tricking. My friend Mickey owned a welding shop. He had welded a tire valve on the side of a beer keg and had attached a high pressure water hose on the other side of the keg. He would fill the tank with water and then pressurize the tank with 120 pounds of air. He would then head to town in his old beat up Galaxy 500 that would withstand a pretty good pelting with eggs. His paint job had been ruined for ten years.

He would crack his window about a quarter of an inch so that it took a perfect shot to get trace amounts of egg in the car. He would then stick the high pressure hose through the quarter inch crack and drench unsuspecting trickers and treaters. This contraption could shoot a stream of water the size of a laser beam the length of a football field.

His car did not have a muffler, so people could hear him coming from a half mile away. After he had been in town for a while and hit people between the eyes a few times with the high pressure stream of water, you would see them run and dive over bushes as they heard him coming in his mufflerless car. Since his name was Mickey, he liked to draw an M on people's chest with the stream of water similar to what Zorro did with his sword.

I know a town should not negotiate with terrorists, but Mickey confirmed to me the chief of police purchased this device from him for two hundred dollars on the condition he would not build another one. I was in the last class of the high pressure spraying tradition on Mount Pleasant Halloween nights.

FLIGHT OF THE FEARLESS ONE

WHEN TOOTERBILL AWOKE in Maury County Hospital with a broken leg and a few busted ribs, he was quite upset with his brother. You couldn't touch Tooterbill anywhere on his body with a powder puff without him squealing in pain. It seems Tooterbill and his brother had been drinking moonshine out at Arrow Lake with Fred Campbell. There was a huge Oak tree beside the bait shop at Arrow Lake that seemed as large as a Redwood Tree. The branches were sprawled out all the way across Arrow Lake Road.

As the three neared the bottom of the bottle of shine, Tooterbill had become convinced that he had the ability to fly. He bet Fred twenty bucks that he could fly from a branch of the Oak tree to the top of the bait shop. It was probably a fifteen foot span. A flying squirrel may have had a chance, but no human could do this . . . not even one that was three quarters deep into a jug of white lightning.

"Why in the world didn't you stop me?" was the question Tooterbill moaned to his brother as he grimaced in pain.

His brother ducked his head with shame when he told Tooterbill, "I thought you could do it. I lost twenty bucks on you too."

Fred was forty dollars richer, but he swears it was like watching the last play of a close football game. He thought for a split second that Tooterbill was going to make it!

THE WRECK

My sister Mary Anna was five years older than me. When I was about eleven years old, our household was awakened by a phone call in the middle of the night. I then heard the worried cry of my mother and the angry words of my dad as they went and looked at a pile of pillows formed in the shape of my sister under the covers of her empty bed. My sixteen year old sister had snuck out of the house by scaling down the gutter pipe just outside of her second story bedroom window. She met up with several of her teenage friends and went for a midnight joy ride. Even at eleven, I was pretty keen on makes and models of cars. Staley Clark had a sharp 58' four-door Chevy.

Carl Lightfoot lived three houses away from us. He was a large red-headed guy of about two hundred and fifty pounds. Carl had never learned how to swim. Porter's Chapel Road dead ends into Campbellsville pike about 6 miles west of town. As Staley approached the stop sign, he never saw it. He was too busy chatting with the other people in the car. Each had parents at home thinking they were sleeping safely in bed.

My sister saw the stop sign pass by her window at forty miles per hour or so and remembers Staley grinning as he was looking towards the back seat after telling one of his stupid jokes. He was unaware that their road had ended. They then went airborne and crashed through a fence row lined with small willow trees. The car, slowed by the fence row, gently rolled upside down on its top in the middle of a creek.

Many small creeks in Tennessee are just a few inches deep and have flat rock bottoms. Fortunately this was one of those creeks. It was summertime and the windows were down. The two inch deep water was now gently flowing through the upside down car which had sustained minimal damage. Seven teenagers were sprawled in various positions inside the car reminiscent of a game of Twister. Mary Anna told me later that there was a strange silence for a few seconds with only a hissing noise coming from the busted radiator and the gentle, peaceful rippling of water through the car. It was kind of like sitting upside down in the serene surroundings of a creek bank. No one was injured at this point and they were in no danger in the shallow creek.

All of a sudden Carl screamed, "I can't swim!" His arms and legs started flailing like a trapped octopus and his huge fist hit Mary Anna square in the forehead. She had never seen arms and legs move that fast. Nobody escaped injury. He slithered out of the car by pushing off of people's faces with his fast moving feet.

My parents came up the driveway with her about three in the morning. My sister's eyes were black and her jaw was swollen, not from the wreck but from Carl. Have you ever seen anyone who looked like they had gone to a stick fight and forgotten their stick? The only one that didn't get hurt was Carl.

My dad did frequent bed checks on both of my sisters from that point on. He took the gutter off of that end of the house and let the water run at will when it rained.

A NIGHT AT TINY'S

WHEN I WAS growing up, my parents would not let me have a motorcycle. The day I turned eighteen I bought a 750 Honda. They were the baddest cycles on the road at the time unless you could afford a Harley. A few weeks later, I decided to join my buddies Hunter and Pie Face and travel three hours south on our motorcycles to attend the Talladega 500 NASCAR race.

We went as far as Birmingham on Saturday and arrived early enough to go out on the town. We ended up somewhere on the west side of town and came upon a white wooden building with no windows and a neon sign that said 'Tiny's'. Several motorcycles were in the parking lot. Well, we had motorcycles so we were one of them. We went inside and each of us ordered a draft and hung out at the bar for a while. It was a quiet, dark place with ten or so people inside. We lasted about thirty minutes before one of us did something that offended a customer. He cursed my buddy, and that of course offended me and my other buddy. The cursing escalated and several of the bikers got up and squared off with us. The situation was now out of control.

The veteran bartender, either because he didn't want his bar torn up or because he didn't want to fill out police reports about three Tennessee boys unconscious on his floor, stepped in with a cool head and calmed everyone down. This made us very happy since we were outnumbered by at least seven. The three of us weighed about four fifty combined. The person that we had offended weighed that much when he had his boots on and he wasn't the biggest one there. His left arm weighed as much as I did.

My dad told me one time that if you are going to have to fight, always pick the biggest person in the room. His reasoning was that you are more than likely going to get whipped anyway and if you get whipped by someone much smaller than you it is hard to show your face for a week or two. If you get whipped by some huge dude you can come to town the next day, battle scars and all and say, "Hey, did ya'll see how big that guy was?" He had a similar theory about why you always use the 21 stick, which is the heaviest stick, when playing pool. In this case, we were too outnumbered and probably would have lost a three on three with these guys, so we didn't have a chance in a ten on three.

As we were led to the door by the bartender, we realized we were getting out of there unscathed. Once we were at the door, we had to show those Alabama boys that we weren't leaving because we were scared and as a matter of fact, they were lucky we were leaving. All three of our chests swelled up and we pointed at them and told them what we would have done had we stayed. Before we gave them time to reply we stepped out of the door and slammed it. Through the thin door, I could hear the cool-headed bartender shuffling and telling his regular patrons to let the idiots leave.

We hurriedly went to our motorcycles and were all three laughing as we mounted up. This was hilarious and we would tell all our bubbas back home about it. It wasn't until we were about to fire up our bikes that we realized we had left our helmets sitting on the bar inside the beer joint.

If there had been a place to buy three helmets we would have shucked out hard earned cash for them before we went back inside. Twenty four hour Wal-Marts were in short supply in Alabama in the late 70's and it was two o'clock on Sunday morning. Alabama had a helmet law and we knew we wouldn't get far bare-headed. We certainly didn't need to get stopped with draft beer on our breath. It was before the age of cell phones and we didn't know anybody in Alabama to come get us anyway. We couldn't even call a tow truck to come get us since the pay phone was inside with our helmets and the big guys. We would also have to go inside and ask to borrow the phone to call the police for protection. We were in one heck of a jam.

The three of us bad boys from Tennessee looked like choir boys when we went back in and strolled straight to the cool-headed bartender. We figured he had a financial stake in getting us out of there alive. I did the talking and in my best squeaky voice said, "May we have our helmets back sir?" He didn't saw a word, nodded his head at the helmets, and turned his back and continued shining a glass.

On the way out, I gently eased the door shut. We went back to the motel and behaved ourselves the rest of the weekend.

THE POLITICIAN

OOTERBILL DECIDED TO run for Constable of Maury County back in the 60's. It was a part time job, but at the time he was unemployed and figured that would give him an edge over the other candidates since he would be available all day to do the tasks of serving papers around the countryside and breaking up fights at Olean's Pool Hall. He had cards printed that read, "Tooterbill for Constable, Unemployed to Serve you Better". Made sense to me, but I was too young to vote at the time.

When Election Day finally came and the results were counted, Tooterbill got one vote. This was a problem. He knew he had voted for himself . . . and he knew his wife had also voted. They had driven to the high school to vote together. If anybody else in the town had voted for him, she wouldn't have been busted. Officer Manley Workman had to break them up in the front yard and take Tooterbill to jail for a cooling off period.

The next morning, the newly elected constable was sworn in, picked Tooterbill up at the jail, gave him all the specifics of his court appearance, and took him home. The new constable had to miss four hours of work at Victor in order to take care of the business he was elected to perform.

THE SWIMMING PARTY

NOBODY LIKES A thief! A rash of home break-ins occurred around my home town back in the late 70's. The homes of known hunters were broken into while they were away and their guns were taken. That should have made the thieves nervous due to the fact that most hunters also have guns in their pickup trucks. Nevertheless, it was an ongoing problem.

They made the mistake of breaking into a fella named Carlton McClain's house. Carlton did a little snooping and passed some hundred dollar bills around town. Pretty soon he had a pretty good lead on who might know something about his guns. I was in the pool room the night they came in and asked Hillbilly Wright to take a ride with them. Hillbilly had been known to steal things or buy stolen things and was known as a low-life even by the low-lifes.

Carlton and his boys escorted the reluctant Hillbilly out and headed west in a convoy of pickup trucks. They took hillbilly to West Fork Creek for an old fashioned baptism, but this one didn't have anything to do with religion. I heard the story from Billy Wayne. He said Carlton asked the question, "Who took my guns?"

Hillbilly's answer was, "I don't know." Carlton put him under for about 30 seconds, then brought him up and repeated the question, "Who took my guns?" After a long inhale, Hillbilly replied, "I don't know."

Billy Wayne said this time when Carlton put him under he waited until Hillbilly stopped bubbling before he brought him back up. Billy Wayne said he got out of breath himself just watching. After Hillbilly gasped and choked and coughed for about 3 minutes, Billy Wayne said he thought they were going to have to slap Hillbilly to get him to shut up. He was rattling names, dates, and places faster than they could write them down.

That night Carlton and his boys started kicking in doors and by morning all his guns were back where they were supposed to be. The gun stealing epidemic subsided in the area. Word travels fast in a small town.

THE METER READER

I RECEIVED A LETTER from the local electric company stating that in an effort to control costs, they were going to start reading my meter every other month rather than the traditional once per month. This system works by estimating the month they skip and adjusting it the next month when they actually take the reading. It cut their meter reader labor and gas in half. Brilliant! Why had nobody thought of this before?

Well, actually they had! Tony Brown was chief meter reader for the city of Mount Pleasant. He had figured out that instead of reading the meters every month he could skip a couple of months, then on the third month just do a little math and make it come out to match what the meter actually read. He could hang out at Olean's Pool Hall instead of doing the tedious, boring job of reading meters. The problem was he was doing this without the blessing of his bosses.

I am sure the local electric company, with this new system of theirs, has some sophisticated formula worked out to account for cold spells and heat waves so people don't get shocked during the months that have the wrath of Mother Nature in them. Tony had not developed such a formula, so when the heat wave of 96' started in early May, it never dawned on Tony that a problem was on the horizon. He had done his quarterly reading in April.

People were tickled pink with their May and June bills, but when Tony actually read the meters in July you could hear the thuds of people hitting the floor when they got their bills. This was the closest my town had come to a riot since 1969.

The city manager stayed busy for weeks answering calls. Although they suspected Tony was doing something to contribute to the problem, it took several months of watching him with binoculars and spot checking meters before they could bust him and fire him.

Tony is now a bartender at Olean's Pool Hall.

THE WELDER

IT IS WELL known that dishonest people steal things from the workplace. It seems the larger the place of employment, the larger the problem. Most people in the world don't steal, but there are bad apples in most sacks. Earl Russell was stealing log chains from Victor Chemical. He would put them in his lunch box and take them out at the end of the day.

One particular day his lunch box pulled free from the handle due to the weight as he walked by the guard shack. It made a sound like the Liberty Bell had rung when it hit the concrete sidewalk. The well intentioned guard reached down to pick up Earl's lunch for him, but could not pick it up with one hand. He knew that either Earl had one heck of a spoon or he was up to no good. Earl was busted and fired. The HR manager finally got one.

I got to know a man named Frank Odom in the 80's. He was an elderly man who had retired from Victor and now piddled part time in construction. He told me that he had worked at Victor for 30 years and was proud of the fact he had never put in a single honest days work. He was not the norm. Most people at Victor work hard and are proud of their company. Frank was proud of the fact that he had been able to steal at least one item every day he worked and had never been caught. He also said he would have worked more than the 30 years he put in, but the plant closed his department because it lost so much money . . . hmmm.

One of Frank's greatest successes he liked to brag about was when he got in a financial bind in the early seventies and had to declare bankruptcy. The lawyer asked him to make a list of all the people he owed and how much he owed them. Frank made the list and gave it to the lawyer. The lawyer had his legal assistant submit the list to the judge. When Frank received the bill from the lawyer, he called the office and informed the legal secretary she should check out their paperwork. It turns out that Frank

110

had put the lawyer's name on the list of people he owed and the legal secretary did not catch it. Frank had taken bankruptcy on the lawyer that filed his bankruptcy. It didn't cost him a dime.

His next greatest success he bragged about was what he considered the one time greatest theft anyone ever perpetrated against Victor Chemical. Most of his daily thefts were small and didn't cost much, but this one was big and expensive. I already knew the story well.

My neighbor, Freddie Hamilton, worked with Frank at Victor and had told me about this incident many times. Freddie didn't agree that it was the biggest one time theft. Freddie claims he stole a pickup truck from the company which out ranked Frank's theft, but said Frank's probably was the second biggest.

Freddie was in the maintenance department and did a lot of welding. A trick that welders play on each other is to turn off each others welding machines while the person is welding. When this happens, the welder first thinks he has lost connection due to flux building up on the end of the welding rod which is a regular occurrence while welding. The welder will bang the end of the rod on the metal a few times in an attempt to get the arc restarted. If that doesn't work, he will then twist the clamp that is attached to the metal to reestablish the connection. When neither of those actions are successful the welder figures out that a prankster has struck and heads to the welding machine to turn it back on.

Freddie went through these processes the morning of July 3rd, 1986. It was such a significant event he remembered the date and the time. He had stolen the pickup truck on February 12, 1978. When Freddie could not get the welder to arc, he grumbled, cursed, and headed towards his welding machine. It had taken him 15 minutes to drag the welding cables to the spot he was welding due to the fact that it was so far from the machine. It was a portable welder on wheels. You've seen them . . . it basically looks like an engine mounted on two wheels so it can be pulled behind a pickup truck.

Freddie went to cut his welder back on hoping to run into the idiot that had cut it off so he could repay him later in the day. When he got to the place he had parked the welder, all that was there was a bolt cutter and the frayed ends of his freshly cut welding cables. He looked up just in time to see Frank heading out of the gate with the welder. He said it was unlike Frank to not steal the bolt cutters also, but he figured he left them as a type of calling card. Frank knew Freddie wouldn't rat him out and the guard at the gate was Frank's brother in law.

The irony is Frank did not know how to weld. He just wanted the welder.

THE USED CAR SALESMEN

KOTCHIE JONES HAD a car lot located near The Z. I ran around with his two boys. His nickname for anybody whose hair touched their ears was 'longhair'. He would always say, "Get me a Pepsi longhair, or hand me that hose longhair . . . etc".

Jeff Waldrup stopped in one afternoon on the way home from work to inquire about a sharp looking step-side pickup truck sitting on Kotchie's lot. When Kotchie told him what he was asking for the truck, Jeff told him he thought it was overpriced and proceeded to walk around the lot looking at the other vehicles. The conversation then turned to Jeff's truck. Kotchie asked if he would sell it and Jeff told him, "Yes, I will." Kotchie asked him what he wanted for the truck and Jeff told him what he would take. Jeff proceeded to stroll around the lot for a little while to see if he would be interested in anything else on the lot. After deciding he was not particularly interested in anything, he told Kotchie, "Well, I guess I'll be heading on home Kotchie."

Kotchie replied, "How are you going?"

A puzzled Jeff asked, "What do you mean?"

Kotchie told Jeff, "I bought your truck fifteen minutes ago!" No amount of arguing from Jeff would change Kotchie's mind. Jeff priced it and Jeff's truck was now Kotchie's truck.

Jeff was an honorable man, so when he couldn't talk Kotchie out of the deal, he reached in his glove box and got the title out. Kotchie paid Jeff and gave him a ride home in Kotchie's new pickup truck.

THE GENIUS

I WENT TO COLLEGE late in life. I took an Ecology course that had a semester project as a requirement. At the time I was living on a farm south of Mount Pleasant. I came up with the ingenious idea of determining squirrel populations based on the type of thicket the little critters lived in for my project. For you city folks, a thicket is a thick growth of trees of the same species. On my farm it was a perfect setup. There were different types of thickets as if it were a giant herbal test tube. There was an oak thicket, and then a few hundred yards away a hickory thicket, then a pine thicket, etc . . . etc . . . A tree scientist (if there is such a thing) could not have had a better place to study.

I proposed this project to my instructor and the class in a 5 minute speech accompanied by overheads and received his blessing to proceed. All I had to do now was go to each thicket, fold out my hunting chair, and count squirrels. One cold January morning, I put on my winter coveralls and headed to the woods. I started with the oak thicket that had a thick carpet of acorns scattered on the ground under the large trees. This would probably be the place the hungry little critters would hang out.

I don't know at exactly what point in the morning the epiphany came to me. The dictionary defines an epiphany as a sudden revelation, sometimes accompanied by a divine being. There was no divine being involved unless it was God's disapproval of the first thought that came to my mind after the revelation. It did not come to me in the first thicket. I switched thickets twice before I realized why I had not seen one squirrel in three and a half hours. Although a tree squirrel does not hibernate the same way a bear does, they become very inactive during the winter months to conserve energy and rarely come out of their nest. In other words, I wasn't able to count any squirrels because they were sleeping in their nests for days at a time.

I finally figured out I could count squirrel *nests* per acre and was able to pull it off with a B. I did somehow graduate from college, but I am not an Ecologist.

THE MISSILE

I DON'T WANT TO beat up on myself too bad, but I have done some really dumb things that would be wasted lessons if not passed along. My good friend Hunter and I decided to start a trucking business in the late seventies. That was dumb in and of itself. We drove them and worked on them, doing the latter the most. We became pretty good shade tree mechanics as we learned from experience. As we worked on them, we didn't receive any injuries worse than skinned knuckles and mashed fingers.

There was one particular day that the previous statement was almost nullified. One of our old rattletrap trucks had run out of fuel in our shop parking lot. When a diesel runs out of fuel the fuel tank has to be pressurized after refilling the tank with fuel to force the fuel back into the fuel line. The fuel line won't start the suction on its own due to having air in the line. I had seen this done a few times, so I took charge. It was Saturday morning and my dad had come up to the shop as he usually did on Saturday to talk and drink coffee.

We had pushed the truck into the shop with a farm tractor to get out of the cold and refilled the tank with diesel. I found a small half inch diameter plug in the top of the tank and took it out so I could insert the high pressure air hose to pressurize the tank. The main fuel cap was made of metal and was 4 inches in diameter. Diesel trucks have much larger openings in the fuel tank than automobiles. A tank with an opening this large that requires air pressure after running out of fuel should have a warning label. The manufacturer had probably never envisioned the following scenario: a large fuel tank, a 2.5 pound fuel cap, a high pressure air line, and two idiots.

I put a rag around the hose as I began pumping air into the tank in order to get as much pressure in the tank as possible. We had twisted the main fuel cap on as tight as it would go so it would hold the pressure in. It was not a threaded cap, but one that you pushed in and twisted a T-handle which in turn put pressure against the side of the opening to hold the cap in. If enough pressure was applied it could slip out.

My dad was standing beside the tank staring at it like men stare at things that are being fixed. My partner, the other idiot besides myself, was sitting in the truck ready to crank the engine on my signal when I felt I had reached a pressure high enough to push the fuel into the fuel line.

I don't have any idea what PSI the tank got to, but I will assure you that the fuel cap manufacturer could have used it in a commercial as much as it withstood. It was at the subatomic level before it gave way. I mentioned I had seen this done, but had never actually done it myself.

We did not even know the cap was gone. We merely heard a loud boom and saw a mist around the opening of the tank. My dad was still staring at the place the fuel cap used to be. We noticed a hissing sound coming out of the hole where the fuel cap used to be. We also noticed there was a hole in the metal roof of the shop that was now letting sunlight in. It was at an angle that corresponded with the direction the fuel tank opening was pointing. As we let what had just happened sink in, we stared at one another with puzzled looks.

The cap had shot out at the speed of a bullet and had gone past my dad's face at 100 meters per second. He didn't even flinch. He never saw it. Just like a bullet leaving a gun barrel, it was just gone.

It is comical now, but we all realized my dad almost died that day.

The next few sentences are exactly as they were stated.

I said, "What was that?"

My partner slowly replied, "Look at that hole in the roof!"

With a puzzled look I said, "Was that the fuel cap?"

Without interjecting an opinion as to what just happened my dad politely said in his slow drawl, "Well boys, I just remembered some things I need to pick up at the feed store, so I reckon I'll see ya'll after while."

He walked out, got in his pickup truck and left. I knew him well enough to know he was actually thinking, "I'm getting out of here before these idiots kill me!" He came around every Saturday for the rest of my trucking career, but never got close to anything we were working on again.

THE SQUARE

ILLY MAC WAS known for being a miser. When Tilly was remodeling his house on Watts Hill, he had borrowed his neighbor's carpenter square to use as a guide and made his own square using two pieces of wood so he wouldn't have to buy a square. If you don't know what a square is, it is one of those metal things that looks like an L. It forms a perfect 90 degree angle. His home-made square worked well until his two boys decided to have a little fun. They pried the nails out and made it a ninety-three degree angle instead of the precise ninety degree angle that Tilly had crafted.

Tilly's next project was building a door in the basement. Once he was finished, the boys swear you had to cock your head slightly to make the door look straight. It was actually leaning 3 degrees. Tilly was a pretty good carpenter and figured out what was wrong. After a thorough investigation and many denials from his sons, they finally confessed to their evil deed.

The boys tore the door out and built him a straight one while Tilly watched from a chair and drank lemonade. He never did buy a store bought square. He simply repaired the one he had.

THE HANGING

WHEN I WAS in the Boy Scouts, I liked to be the troop clown. I was always scheming up something to make the other boys laugh. This particular day while my buddies were in knot tying class, I had tied a knot of my own. I tied a hangman's noose around my ankle and threw the rope over a tree branch that was about ten feet off of the ground. I was going to pull myself up by my foot, hang upside down, and then yell for my buddies to see this feat . . . excuse the pun. Have you ever tried hoisting yourself up by the foot? Don't!

My first two or three pulls went ok. My left leg was curling up behind my back with each pull. My right foot was still planted firmly on the ground, so no problem yet. I had amazing balance in those days, so my left leg was well above the back of my head before I had to make the tug that took my right foot off of the ground which meant neither foot remained on the ground. As soon as I made this final tug, I was upside down and spinning out of control. I was holding firmly onto the rope to keep from dropping on my head. The problem was the rope had somehow wrapped about three quarters of the way around my neck. It was now choking me, so I had no choice but to let go.

I headed the two feet back to earth at thirty two feet per second per second. The friction from the rope took a two inch by four inch layer of the skin off of my neck. I was now a twelve year old boy lying on the ground thankful to be alive. Nobody had seen a thing. I stumbled down to the other group. When twelve year olds cry, they can't talk. They can only whimper and point, which I did.

After I gained my composure, I was able to explain myself to my buddies, but as usual when most of them got home they told their parents the more exciting version of how Marshall had tried to hang himself. Word travels fast in a small town. I got a lot of looks at my huge scab for the next couple of weeks. I never made another hangman's noose and have always kept both feet planted on the ground since that fateful day.

THE EAGLE

I WENT TO WORK at a local company in the maintenance department when I was in my twenties. One of the guys I worked with was named Greg. He was around thirty years old. To a guy in his early twenties, a thirty year old is an old man and assumed to be wise. Greg was neither old nor wise.

We had a small electric chain hoist in the shop used for lifting heavy things. It was suspended on a rail about fifteen feet above the shop floor and was operated by a handheld control that hung from the hoist by a coil of wire similar to a telephone cord. It had up, down, and sideways buttons. About twice a week when the supervisor left for lunch, Greg would take the chain and hook it to his belt just above his rump. He would operate the crane by the handheld control and hoist himself to the ceiling of the shop. He would then proceed to flap his arms and squawk like an eagle. I laughed as much the twentieth time I saw him do this as I did the first time. He kept the control in his hand so he could let himself back down when he was done with his foolishness.

One day, just as Greg got to the top and was flapping his wings and making his classic squawking noise, the supervisor walked into the shop. He had forgotten something and had come back early from his lunch break to retrieve it.

Did he write Greg up for unsafe shop practices? No! He walked directly to the electrical breaker box and flipped off the breaker that controlled the electric chain hoist. The down button no longer worked. Greg begged him to turn the breaker back on until he could no longer talk. The last couple of requests were gentle mumbles.

Greg was now limp and bent double, just hanging there like a bat. His arms and legs were dangling straight towards the floor like a dead man in the old western movies draped across a saddle. He had long since dropped the control device. We finally talked the supervisor into turning the breaker back on. We lowered Greg to the floor using the hand held control, took the hook off of his belt, and let him lie there. He remained on the floor for about an hour, and then slowly got up. He didn't say anything to anyone. He just staggered outside, got in his pickup truck, and slowly left the parking lot in the direction of his house.

The next morning he came in as usual and had the normal half-smile on his face. He went into the supervisor's office and closed the door. After a ten minute meeting, he came out and was business as usual for the rest of the day. They had come to an understanding about unauthorized use of the company chain hoist.

No matter how much I begged and pleaded Greg the rest of the time I worked there, I never could persuade him to raise himself up with the hoist again. I think Greg grew up a little that day!

THE 4 INCH SPIDER

WHEN MY WIFE and I first got married in the late 70's, we rented a little farm house sitting on the edge of a corn field near The Z. It had been vacant for a couple of years, so we had to do quite a bit of dusting and cleaning before we could move in.

We were excited about our 900 square foot house as most newlyweds are. I was lucky enough to get the first bath the night we moved in. The house didn't have a shower, just an old cast iron claw foot bath tub. We had given the tub a good scrubbin', so I ran a steamy tub of water and got in. Everything was fine until it came time to wash my hair.

Up until this point, only about 180 pounds worth of my 200 pound body was displacing water. I am estimating my head to weigh twenty pounds with my neck attached. When my head went under the water, the water level was raised high enough to flow into the overflow drain. My knees had come out of the water forming islands as I slid my head under the water. As my head was still submerged, I felt a strange sensation on my left knee.

If you ever move into an old farm house and clean the bathtub sparkling clean, don't forget to check the overflow drain. I slowly raised my eyes above the water level and looked at my knee with my nose still submerged, kinda like those special ops guys come out of the water. There was a purple spider sitting on my knee staring me directly in the eyes. I am sure it was in the Tarantula family . . . had to be. It had a four inch leg span and it was not a Daddy Long Legs!

The moment I saw it, it bit me. I jumped straight up in the air, and while I was in the air, I went sideways about two feet and somehow landed on my feet beside the tub. Most of the water in the tub came with me. The spider also came with me. I squalled like a dog that had touched an electric fence.

My wife would never swear on a Bible that this spider was four inches across or that my head weighs twenty pounds, but she would swear that I kept that spider in a jar on top of the refrigerator for a week. I gave her instructions that if I passed out she was to hand it to the ambulance driver and say, "This is what got him."

We thoroughly cleaned the overflow drain before it was my wife's turn to get a bath.

THE 4 CENTIMETER SPIDER

OST OF THE teenage population of Mount Pleasant was at some point in their early life employed at Butch's Market. It was a great after school and summer job. Butch Sisk was the owner and was well loved by all of the people of Mount Pleasant. I did a stint there when I was sixteen. I was trained by a guy nicknamed Bloop. He was a nut. The day I started working there, Bloop showed me a very realistic looking black plastic spider he had purchased at Couch's Dime Store. He carefully placed it behind a can of chili beans so that an unsuspecting customer would get the surprise of their life.

I had no idea of the extent of his plan. I noticed he would always act like he was stocking things in the area of the chili beans when customers would come down the aisle. I just thought he wanted to see the reaction close up. About two hours after he had put the spider behind the can, an elderly lady with blue hair stopped by the chili beans. She picked up the can and screamed when she saw the spider. Bloop, who happened to be two feet away, yelled, "A spider, I've got it!" He quickly grabbed it, put it in his mouth, and actually swallowed the plastic spider. He told the lady, "We've been having a problem with those, but I eat them as fast as I can find them."

The elderly lady looked at him with a disgusting look, and then pushed her cart down the aisle looking back over her shoulder at him every ten feet or so as she shook her head. She appeared to be mumbling to herself. She knew she had just come in contact with a real weirdo.

I also looked at him with disgust. I had the knowledge that she did not have that this was just a plastic spider, but I also knew she had come in contact with a real weirdo. I got to know many of the customers during my time at Butch's market, but never saw this lady again.

THE DYNAMITE EXPERTS

I F YOU GOT to the west end of The Z and kept going straight you would end up on Dry Creek Road. It is a picture perfect setting meandering south towards the Alabama line. The steep hills are dotted by grazing cattle and horses. This is a place where an artist could set up an easel and spend a day brushing in the scenery. If an artist had been there on this particular hot summer day, he or she would have needed plenty of white paint for smoke effects. The next thing the artist would have needed to do is grab his or her easel and run for cover.

I was eighteen and working for a pipeline construction company putting a water line down the side of Dry Creek Road. My coworkers and I would drill holes in the solid rock with a jackhammer, drop a stick of dynamite in each hole, and pack dirt into the holes over the dynamite to keep the dynamite from simply blowing back out of the hole without cracking the rock. We would then walk down the road the length of a football field to an old country store, buy a Dr Pepper and a Moon Pie, and wait for a guy named Willie to shoot the dynamite off. This was a daily process. The blast would be set off just before lunch, and then backhoes would dig the broken rock out of the ditch the rest of the day as we laid pipe behind them.

Before the charge was set off each day, one of the front-end loader operators would place a dynamite mat on top of the blast area to keep dirt and rock from flying in the air. You've probably seen these mats near construction sites on the side of the road. They are about ten feet square and are made up of old rusty steel cables meshed together like a giant knitted potholder.

We had set off at least a hundred charges in the months we had been on the job and each one was the same. The ground would tremble with a simultaneous muffled rumble. The dynamite mat would rise about 6 inches, and then settle back down in a small cloud of dust and smoke. The sound of machinery would then crank back up as the operators removed the mat and got ready for the afternoon dig.

This particular day, we were re-drilling the holes from the previous day. We had hit a stretch of rock that contained a lot of loose seams. Dynamite follows the path of least resistance like electricity and the charge was blowing out of the seams and not cracking the solid rock. After we got new holes drilled, our foreman told us to drop two sticks in each hole instead of the customary one stick. This made sense to us so we did as he said. Just as we were about to start packing dirt into the holes over the dynamite, he came into the ditch with a fifty pound sack of ammonium nitrate and told us to pack the holes with the powdery white substance instead of dirt.

Ammonium nitrate was normally used as fertilizer, but he had read in a book that it would add to the explosive kick of the dynamite when soaked with diesel fuel. After the holes were packed with the ammonium nitrate, he pulled the fuel truck next to the ditch and poured diesel fuel over each hole allowing it to saturate the powdery white chemical. We then went thru the normal routine of filling the ditch with dirt to keep the rocks from going airborne. After finishing, we walked down to the old country store to get our snacks as the operators placed the mat on top of the blast area.

Just as I opened the old wooden screen door of the store, I heard the foreman yell at an operator to pull a bulldozer to the mat and lock the blade down on top of the mat in order to help hold the blast down since the blast would have a little more kick than usual. We had never done this before but it sounded like a heck of an idea to me. After all, we had the holes packed with twice as much dynamite and had added a little extra kick of ammonium nitrate.

As I came out of the store and sat down on the wooden steps to have my refreshments, everything looked normal. Willie, the guy that always set the charges off by touching the wires of the dynamite cord to a car battery, was rolling the cable out and preparing to set off the charge. His cord was about fifty feet long which was pretty close to the dynamite, but all the charge ever did was rumble a little and create a small dust cloud . . . so no problem. He knelt down on one knee as always and I saw him touch the wire to the battery out of the corner of my eye.

Instead of the normal rumble, it sounded as if an atomic bomb had gone off. I immediately snatched my head in the direction of the blast and witnessed the bulldozer flipping over backwards. The dynamite mat was spiraling upward and looked as if it had been sent into orbit. Willie was bouncing down the road on his back like somebody had skipped him like a rock in a creek. My coworker and I looked like the two stooges as our heads and eyes slowly followed the tons of rock and dirt that had been thrown into the air and were forming a rainbow arch that slowly started falling back to earth in all directions including where we were sitting.

We watched the huge rocks in unbelief for a few seconds before reacting. When we did react, it was simultaneous. We both dropped our refreshments and scrambled under the old wooden porch of the store. All the other workers that had been standing around the construction site were diving under things as if we were in an air raid.

It is strange the way the rocks fell. I guess a physicist could explain this better than me. At first a few pebbles started dropping around us. We heard them pelting the tin roof of the store like a heavy rain. Then basketball size rocks started thudding the ground around us. We could hear rocks going through the roof of the store and splintering the wooden floor inside. Then four or five refrigerator size rocks started pounding the ground. One of these huge rocks buried into the road about ten feet from a dazed and confused Willie who was still lying on his back with the dynamite cord in his hand.

High voltage power lines were directly above where we had set off the charge. The dynamite mat had gone upwards between the wires and was now tangled in the wires like a kite. Once the smoke and dust cleared, we could see that the bulldozer was a tangled mess of steel. It looked like it had been blown up by a roadside bomb. I guess technically it had been.

The ambulance came and took Willie away. All he could do was open his mouth and babble. His vocal cords did not seem to work. He was skinned up a little bit, but the trip to the hospital was mainly for his psychological condition. The second ambulance took the store owner. He was as old as the store and did not attempt to talk. He just followed them where they led him. He had sat in a recliner next to the cash register with a blank stare on his face until the ambulance got there.

For the next few days, there were no charges set off. There were a lot of people at the construction site in suits carrying note pads asking questions. Most of us laborers stayed on our hands and knees the rest of the week picking up rocks from the neighbors' yards and pastures. The neighbors were kind enough to walk around and point out any pebbles we had missed.

The store owner regained his senses in a couple of days and had the ability to speak now . . . very loudly. I am sure this incident cost the construction company owners their profits that were expected from the job, but the charge did bring the stubborn rock out of the ditch so we could continue installing the pipeline southbound towards the Alabama line.

It's a Jungle Out There

PICTURE THIS: YOU are eleven years old and watching Gilligan's Island reruns after school. A friend from down the street calls and says, "Come down here as fast as you can, there's a monkey in the dog pen!" If you grew up in Africa that would not be a big deal, but since I grew up in Tennessee I did what most eleven year old Tennesseans would have done and said, "OK, I'll be down there in a minute or two." I then hung up the phone, sat back down on the couch, and continued drinking my Ski and watching Gilligan. Al Hardison had pulled a few good tricks on me in the past, so I wasn't falling for this one.

Not to get off track, but every time I watched an episode of Gilligan's Island as a youngster I honestly believed that this would be the day they would get off that stupid island. Gilligan would always mess it up in the last five minutes of the show. I despise Gilligan to this day.

Al called again, "Where are you, hurry, there's a monkey in the dog pen!" Ok, I'll bite. I started towards Al's house which was two houses away from my house. I went around corners cautiously in case this was an ambush by Al and some of the neighborhood cronies. Al was a couple of years older, so he did have a tendency to pick on the younger kids every now and then. When I came around the corner of his house, I could see the dog pen that was built in the woods at the edge of his back yard. I saw him flailing his arms and pointing at something. I now broke from my meandering walk and sprinted the next twenty five yards to the dog pen. There was a little 2 foot tall monkey in the dog pen!

Al's dad, known by all the kids in the neighborhood as Uncle Alan, had built this pen for his bird dogs. It had chicken wire spread over the top so they could not climb out. The monkey had somehow gotten into the pen, probably after the dog food, and now could not find the hole he had used for his (or her?)

129

entrance. The monkey was in the corner shivering. Duke the bird dog was in the other corner shivering.

The first thing we did was carefully open the door of the pen and get Duke out. That was easy. Duke was ready to get away from the monkey. We then got a plastic clothes basket out of the laundry room of Al's house and a piece of plywood from Uncle Alan's workshop. We entered the pen and proceeded to corner the monkey. That monkey could literally run on the walls of the pen like a race car rides on the steep banks of a race track.

After about thirty minutes of chasing this monkey around the ten foot square pen our tongues were hanging out as was the monkey's tongue. The monkey was squealing, the dog was barking, and we were screaming. We finally got the clothes basket over the monkey. We slid the piece of plywood under the upside down clothes basket and the monkey and put a concrete block on top of the clothes basket so the monkey could not get out. We took the trapped monkey into Al's basement and called Uncle Alan and asked him to come home because "We have a monkey in the basement." When twenty minutes or so had gone by and he hadn't arrived, Al called him back. He was just like me . . . he had been tricked before. He didn't believe the story and was still in town. At Al's begging, he begrudgingly came home.

We already had a name picked out for our new pet. We were going to call him (or her?) Gilligan. Unfortunately, Uncle Alan hauled the monkey off in the trunk of his car and we never saw Gilligan again. It turns out the monkey was an escaped pet from a house about three blocks away. We often wondered what else lived in the woods behind our houses . . . lions or tigers or bears? Anything was possible now.

THE BUZZARDS

I WILL NEVER FORGET a scene from a movie I saw twenty years or so ago. A man and his wife were standing in front of a two story house with their realtor deciding whether or not this was the house of their dreams. All of a sudden a small airplane, sputtering as if it had run out of fuel, crashed into the house demolishing the second story. The gentleman, pondering on whether to buy the house or not, immediately said, "We'll take it! The odds of another airplane ever hitting this house are astronomical!"

It wasn't long after seeing this movie that I decided to take flying lessons. The movie wasn't my inspiration . . . only a coincidence. My flight instructor was a former Norwegian fighter pilot named Earl who had settled in Mount Pleasant for some reason. It is a great place to settle down, but how does someone from Norway end up there?

I never realized you had to actually stall the airplane out to learn how to fly it. This scared the heck out of me every time we did it. On my third lesson, I was practicing a stall when all of a sudden Earl grabbed the controls and said, "Let me have it!" He rolled the plane over into a dive. As we picked up speed in the dive, the noise sounded just like it does in the movies when a plane is in an uncontrolled dive. I was pinned back in my seat and petrified.

He smacked a buzzard with the left wing. It was a perfect shot and it was evident he had practiced this many times. I never knew buzzards had that many feathers. He pulled out of the dive in his best John Wayne fashion as the airplane shook . . . gritting his teeth and cursing the airplane. We came out of it just above the treetops. He looked over at me grinning and said, "I hate those darn things."

From that day on, after learning this was a dangerous obsession he had, my goal was to avoid buzzards at all costs. If I saw buzzards circling in the east, I flew west. I was glad the day I made my first solo flight. This meant I didn't have to fly with Earl any longer!

131

THE ELEVATOR

WHEN MY OLDEST son Marc was ten years old, he became petrified of elevators. When we were required to ride an elevator, he would stop outside and have to be slid in like a reluctant dog on a leash. On this particular day we had driven to Nashville to attend an event at Municipal Auditorium. We parked in the parking garage and had a choice of walking down four stories or taking the elevator. I knelt down on one knee and told my trusting ten year old how elevators were safe and only got stuck in the movies. After all, I was in my thirties and had never been stuck on one.

I finally gained his trust and convinced him of this, so he reluctantly got on the elevator with us. When the door opened on the ground floor the elevator was stuck halfway between floors. To steal a Charlie Daniels' line, he 'let out a yell that would curl your hair!'

There was a family standing on the outside that was evidently familiar with this elevator. They assured us and our son that the elevator did this all the time. They helped us climb out of the elevator one at a time, and then to our amazement the man crawled up into the elevator and helped his wife and son crawl in. We could only see him from the waste down when he stood up, but he pushed the button and nonchalantly stood there as the door closed. I guess they made it where they were going.

When we returned from the event, we took the stairs to the fourth floor to get our car. My grown son claims he still has a thing about elevators. He is sure he would have grown out of his original illogical fear, but when what he thought could happen actually happened, it left a mental scar. He usually takes the steps.

THE LITTLE PERSON

FATTY ISABELL WAS pretty tough back in his younger days. He weighed about 350 pounds and had been known to get into some scrapes at Olean's Pool Hall. One muggy summer night he was going to see a movie at the Mount Pleasant Theater. The theater sat on the town square and has long since been torn down, but I can remember going as a child. It seems like we always had to stand in line to get in.

This particular night, an adult little person cut line in front of Fatty. The top of this man's head came to Fatty's belt buckle. Thinking he would impress his date, Fatty reached and grabbed the man's shirt at both of his shoulders, picked him up by his shirt, and set him out of line. To make matters worse, Fatty kicked him in the rear. This was the straw that broke the camel's back.

This three and a half foot tall man reached up and grabbed Fatty's belt buckle with his left hand and jumped up and put his feet on Fatty's knees. He looked like a rock climber hanging onto Fatty. He then started hitting Fatty in the face so fast he looked like Rocky Balboa. This little person brought the big man down right there on the town square.

Fatty learned a lesson that night and would have been much better off picking on someone his own size.

THE LICENSE CHECK

IN THE LATE 70's I drove an old Chevy pickup truck. I kept it parked in my driveway which was surrounded by oak trees. One night, two of my buddies and I pulled into a convenience store in Columbia to get some 'refreshments'. From time to time, the starter on my truck would overheat and I would have to either wait on the starter to cool off or beg for a jump from a passerby to get restarted. I kept a set of jumper cables in the bed of the truck for just such occasions.

When I came out of the store this particular night and tried to crank the engine, it only clicked. Since we didn't know anyone in the parking lot to ask for a jump, we decided to just sit and sip on our refreshments as the starter cooled off.

There had been a rash of convenience store robberies around the county recently and I guess when the clerk saw us sitting in the parking lot for a longer than necessary period of time she called the police.

Three squad cars screeched to a halt on three sides of us and we were asked to step out of the vehicle. We quickly complied and answered a few questions as to why we were just sitting in the parking lot. I explained to the officer about my starter problems and told him that I had jumper cables in the bed of the truck.

This is where the confusion began. I could have sworn the officer said, "Could I see them, please", referring to the jumper cables. I said "sure" and stepped over to the bed of my truck to produce the jumper cables. After all, nobody would ever lie about whether or not they possessed a set of jumper cables.

It was fall of the year and the oak trees that I parked under had shed their leaves about a foot deep in the truck bed, thus covering the jumper cables that I needed to produce to prove we were not robbers. As I was feeling around in the leaves trying to locate the jumper cables, the pressure was mounting since our whole story, which happened to be the truth, depended on these jumper cables existing in the truck bed.

After thirty seconds of not being able to locate them, I moved to the other side of the truck as my heart rate increased in panic. Little beads of sweat were forming on my forehead. I nervously explained, "I know they are in here somewhere!"

I noticed that the officers were looking at each other with a puzzled look on their face. Stranger than that, my two friends were looking at me with that 'what in the world are you doing' look. One of the officers looked at my friend Pie Face and said, "Is this where he usually keeps his drivers license?"

Upon hearing that statement, my mind rewound all of the statements that had been made in the last five minutes or so. I realized that very shortly before his statement, "Could I see them, please" we had also talked about my license. Everybody present knew that this was what the request was for except me. The officers thought I was either being a smart aleck or was on dope and the more I tried to explain that I had misunderstood him, the more I sounded like I was on dope. I quit looking for the jumper cables. He did not care a lick if the jumper cables were there and wasn't going to give us a jump anyway.

The officer checked my license which I had produced at the speed of light and then asked me to try to start the car. For the first time in my life I was praying that it wouldn't start. It cranked as if it was on the showroom floor at Lucas Chevrolet. The officer looked at me over the top of his glasses and handed my license back to me. He turned around without saying a word, got in his car, and drove off. The other officers gave me a disgusting look, shook their heads, and left also. I had a feeling we had better be gone when they came back by, so we headed back to the safety of The Z where we knew all of the officers of the law and felt a little safer.

I went to Rippey Auto parts the next morning and bought a new starter on credit.

THE HUNDRED DOLLAR CHICKENS

S INCE I WAS not a full time farmer, I did everything a farmer does, but I only did it about one tenth as much. Most farmers at some point in their life have raised chickens. When my oldest son Marc came home from elementary school one day with a 4H project to raise these yard birds, it sounded like a heck of an idea to me. It would give him lessons in responsibility and economics.

We proceeded to the local farm supply store to purchase what we needed to hatch and raise these chickens. By the time we left the store we had left most of my pay check, but we had enough cages and lights to incubate a baby hippopotamus. I guess I thought the main expense was over, but every Saturday morning my son and I headed to the farm supply store to buy what we needed to keep these confounded chickens alive for another week.

Now don't get me wrong, it is good to spend quality time with your children, but I found out there are cheaper ways to do it. By now we had built a chicken coup and had furnished it with enough hay to feed that hippo I was just talking about. I had covered the outside area with chicken wire to keep my lunatic bird dog out and had mixed and shoveled concrete into holes around the bottom to keep the foxes out.

Many of the full time farmers hung out at the farm supply store on Saturday mornings. They loved to see Marc and I come in each week so they could rib me about this chicken project. One rainy Saturday morning, I went in to buy more chicken feed. It was particularly crowded since the farmers had been rained out of their daily chores. Ole man Grissom asked me in his gruff voice, "McGaw, how you boys doing with those chickens?"

"Alright, I guess," I responded.

"Would you be interested in selling one or two of them?" he laughingly asked.

"Yes sir, I think we would," was my reply.

"How much would you have to have for them?" he asked as he grinned and cut his eyes at his fellow full-time farmers who were also chuckling.

"Well, I tell you what Mr. Grissom, to break even I would have to have a hundred dollars apiece for them"! I said this knowing you can buy a chicken for five bucks.

I never cracked a smile, paid my bill, and walked out. Some were laughing, others were wondering if I was serious or not. A hundred dollars was a heck of an exaggeration, but if I had sold them for fifty dollars apiece I would have lost money . . . and that's the truth. My son and I were in a classic state of being 'upside down' in the business world. We had much more invested than what the yard birds were worth.

THE BUSINESSMAN

I WANTED TO USE these chickens to teach my son about the way commerce worked. Once the hens started laying eggs, my son went to the surrounding neighbors and established an egg route. Each time he would raid the chicken coup for a dozen eggs, he would take them to one of these neighbors and sell them for a dollar a dozen. After three weeks or so, he had saved ten dollars. He would take the money out a couple of times each night and count it.

The following Saturday morning I told him, "Get up son, it's time to go to the farm supply store to get feed for your chickens." When we arrived at the farm supply store I told Ferris Pettus that we needed a fifty pound bag of hen scratch. He went to the back, got the hen scratch, rang it up on the 1920's era cash register, and said, "That'll be three dollars boys."

I told my son, "OK son, pay the man for your feed."

My little entrepreneur could not believe these chickens had now cost him money. No matter how many times I showed him that he still had seven dollars left, he could not get over the fact they had cost him three dollars.

On the way back to the farm he said, "Daddy, I've decided I don't want to raise chickens any longer. I want to sell them to Mr. Grissom."

THE HOSPITAL

I WAS TRAVELLING BACK to Maury County from west Tennessee on a Saturday afternoon when I became ill. I decided that I felt bad enough to seek medical help. There were no doctor's offices open, so I decided to go to an emergency room. I saw a hospital sign on a street corner with an arrow pointing west, so I turned west. After making a few blocks, I knew I was lost. I saw a farm supply store and knew that I could get some information from a friendly face.

I went in and asked the manager where I was going wrong in my pursuit of the hospital. He raised his eyebrows and looked over his glasses at me with a look of seriousness. "What's wrong with you boy?" he asked very slowly.

"Well, I'm having severe stomach pains."

With a serious look on his face he told me, "Maury County Hospital is about an hour east of here. If you think you can make it there, that's what you need to do . . . but if you think you are going to die before you get there, go out this road for about a mile and stop when you see Dr. George's name on the mailbox. He is the county veterinarian, but knows more about medicine than any doctor in our county. He will patch you up enough to get you to Maury County. If you go to our hospital, you will more than likely die even if you weren't going to before going there."

I went back outside, got in my pickup truck, and headed to Maury County. I was feeling much better by the time I crossed the Maury County line and headed home to The Z instead of Maury County Hospital.

THE WRESTLING MATCH

NORMI AND CHIC Williams were brothers and ran a trucking company on the east side of Mount Pleasant. Normi lived on The Z and told me a story one time that was as hilarious watching him tell it as it was trying to picture it in my mind. When he and Chic were teenagers in the early fifties, they were trying to impress some young females at the Maury County fair. They came upon a wrestling ring with a sign that said 'Win twenty dollars if you can pin the monkey'. Normi was pretty wiry and felt like he had a good shot at accomplishing the goal. He paid the ringmaster fifty cents and climbed into the ring.

The monkey was concealed in a shed about the size and shape of an outhouse on the side of the ring. He could hear the monkey making grunting noises and banging against the door like he wanted out. When the ringmaster let him out, it was actually a five foot tall baboon. Normi squared up in his best wrestling stance in preparation to wrestle this ape and assumed the ape would wrestle with him. The ape drew his fist back like George Foreman and stunned Normi with a right hook. When Normi hit the ground, the baboon straddled the stunned Normi and pinned him in about 2.5 seconds after the match started.

Chic, thinking this was not fair that the ape was using fists, entered the ring. The ringmaster was yelling at Chic to get out. Chic jumped on the ape's back. The surprised ape jumped up and started turning circles and making those noises that baboons make. Chic's legs were sticking out parallel to the mat like kid's legs do when their older brothers spin them around in the yard. The ape eventually slung Chic off and managed to get him in a headlock. Normi was just regaining his senses and now pounced on the ape's back. The ape started his spin move with Normi.

Chic, who had not been stunned by a right hook, was able to jump on the ape from his blind side. The ape was punching both of them like a boxer. They managed to get the ape on the mat and get his arm twisted behind him so they could push his

140

hand towards the back of his shoulder blade to keep him down. Have you ever had anybody do you that way? It will make you comply.

The problem now was they had a captured ape. It is like catching a snake with your hand. Once you have caught it, it is hard to let go without getting bitten. They didn't know how to let this berserk monkey go. The irate ringmaster was pulling on both of them, so they let go of the monkey and sprinted into the crowd without their twenty bucks they felt like they had just won. The ringmaster was still yelling at them in what they think was Romanian and the monkey was still squealing.

They headed back to Mount Pleasant, but had a tale to tell for the rest of their lives about the time they pinned the boxing monkey. They were sure the monkey had never been pinned before since he usually knocked his unsuspecting opponents out with the first lick.

CECIL THE DIESEL

ALTHOUGH A SMALL town, Mount Pleasant has always been loaded as far as high school sports go. In the late 50's the football team at Hay Long High School had a line that looked like the Tennessee Vols. One of the members of that line was Cecil the Diesel. He weighed in at 350 pounds. After high school, Cecil started hanging out with some boys from Lewis County which is never a good thing.

They came up with a heck of an idea. They would break into country stores at night and would not have to work for a living. This was in the days when most of the front doors of the old country stores were solid wood. Cecil would get a twenty foot running start, lower his shoulder, and bust the door down. The future felons that were witnesses to this said it was amazing. They claimed if you stood near the doors when he hit them, splinters would stick in you from ten feet away.

They hit ole' man Caffey's store on Hampshire Pike one night, but ole' man Caffey was asleep behind the counter with his double barrel twelve gauge. He held them at gunpoint until the sheriff got there. Every store that had been burglarized by having the front door knocked down was pinned on this gang.

After eleven months and twenty-nine days in Maury County jail, Cecil was a changed man and to my knowledge has not missed a Sunday in church since.

THE CROSS EYED BIRD DOG

As a boy, I loved to go quail hunting with my dad in the fall of the year. We would tromp through the freshly cut corn fields, careful not to trip over the six inch tall brown stalks sticking out of the ground. We would then cross fences into fields of knee high sagebrush. All the while we were hoping one of the bird dogs would lock up in a point position pointing at a covey of quail. We would always go with Uncle Alan. A few months back Uncle Alan had stumbled upon a prize bird dog that had a championship bloodline. He got a heck of a deal on the dog because the dog was cross-eyed. When you looked him in the eyes, one eye would stare back at you and the other eye would be looking about five feet to the right.

He was the best bird dog I had ever seen as far as finding the quail, but many times when he was pointing he would actually be five feet to the left of the covey. When he jumped in to flush the quail they would fly up about five feet to the right of where he was pointing. It was a challenge for the shooters to adjust to that position after being prepared to shoot towards the spot he had pointed. They could not compensate and simply prepare to shoot five feet to the right because half the time the dog was right on the money. It seems he saw double and could not differentiate between the real vision and the fake vision. He tried to jump into the bed of Uncle Alan's pickup truck one day and planted his nose square into his left blinker.

One afternoon one of the other dogs was in a point stance. My dad and Uncle Alan were easing towards the spot to get ready for the dog to flush the birds out. Out of nowhere came Uncle Alan's dog at thirty miles per hour. He ran square into the back legs of Uncle Alan and sent him and his Browning twenty gauge sprawling towards the ground. The dog had picked the wrong vision. After the ribbing Uncle Alan took over this event, he sold his champion. Hunting was still fun, but was never the same after that.

THE SKIER

WHEN MY OLDEST son Marc was in high school, he talked me into going to the Sea Doo dealership and buying a jet ski. One of the things the salesman touted about the unit we were interested in was that it was powerful enough to pull a person on water skis. Thinking back, I don't think he actually said to try it, just that it was possible. I had not been skiing since going to the Tennessee River with my buddies when I was in high school. I bought the jet ski, climbed into the attic to retrieve my old Cypress Gardens skis, and headed to the lake.

Since my son had never been skiing, I volunteered to go first. There is an art to pulling someone on skis. I had learned it in my many trips to the river. The problem was not only had my son never been skiing, he had never pulled a skier. I proceeded to give him a five minute crash course on how to pull me down the river.

Another thing the salesperson had told us was this jet ski would go fifty-five miles per hour. All the skiing I had previously done had been behind a sixty-five horsepower Mercury outboard at thirty-five miles per hour. If you have ever done any waterskiing, thirty-five miles per hour is plenty fast for anyone that is not a professional skier.

I knew that he would have to give it all the power the engine had to initially pull my 200 pound frame out of the water, so I instructed him to get me up with full throttle. I told him once I was up to look back and watch for my signal. I would give him the thumb down when I wanted him to slowly decrease the speed down to the thirty-five mile per hour mark. If he decreased too quickly, the rope would go slack and I would simply sink.

When he hit the gas, it surprisingly snatched me up out of the water in a couple of seconds. We went from zero to fifty-five in another two seconds. I had never been on a set of skis going this fast and my jaws were expanding and quivering from the air going in my mouth. When I closed my mouth the wind still blew my lips apart exposing my teeth.

The lake was a little choppy, so I was now holding on for dear life. My son would look around as I had instructed him, but would have to quickly look back forward in order to watch out for other watercraft. I would manage to let go with one hand for a split second and quickly give the thumb down, but the rope would start whipping the water and I would have to grab it again with my signaling hand. I was trying to time my split second hand signal with his split second turnaround.

We went about a quarter of a mile at fifty-five and then went over the wake of another boat. At this point I went air-born. It was not the classic air-born that you see when watching water skiing on television. It would be more like watching a combination of Olympic diving and rock skipping.

When I hit the water face forward, the first three or four bounces didn't hurt. It was when my velocity slowed down enough for me to actually go into the water instead of skipping along the surface that it hurt. Water shot up my nose at forty miles per hour. I remember seeing my right toe about one inch in front of my eyeball as my right foot rested on the top of my head as if I were a contortionist.

When I finally stopped and came back to the surface, I could see the jet ski heading off into the sunset at fifty-five miles per hour with the rope handle bouncing along the surface of the water behind it. My son had not done his split second turnaround to see if I was still back there. When he finally noticed I was gone and came back he said, "It took me a few minutes to find you!"

I tried to climb onto the back of the jet ski so he could take me back to shore, but my legs would only wobble when I tried to put any weight on them to pull up. I finally told him to idle in. I held onto the back of the jet ski and let him drag me to shore. All of my son's high school buddies were there. They said I looked like a person that had been shipwrecked as I crawled up on the shore. It took me 15 minutes or so to recover. I then asked my son if he wanted to ski next.

He politely responded, "No thanks, dad." I made the offer to all of his buddies but had no takers.

As I think back on this treasured memory of my kid's childhood, and my attempt at a second childhood, one thing always enters my mind. Why didn't I just let go of the rope? Do you think you would have thought of that? Don't be so sure. When your brain is fighting for survival, it is not easy to think of all your options.

THE FIRST DATE

Y MOST MEMORABLE disaster on New Years Eve was my first date with the girl of my dreams who would eventually become my wife. I had a 1974 Chevy Vega. If you aren't old enough to remember the Vega, it was Chevrolet's failed attempt to put a car on the market that resembled a muscle car, but did not guzzle gas. Yes, we were worried about gas mileage in the early seventies when gas climbed to an outrageous fifty cents a gallon. The Vega had the first aluminum block four cylinder engine. The ultimate test of this engine was a seventeen year old in a small Tennessee town cruising The Z. The engine lasted about six months.

My friend's dad owned Griggs Chevrolet in Mount Pleasant. He brought me some literature on replacing the four cylinder engine with an eight cylinder. I bought a Doug Thorley conversion kit and we spent the next twenty or so nights converting my little compact car into a real muscle car. It was hilarious to pull up beside a Camaro or Mustang at a stop light and blow them away when the light turned green. They would usually flash their lights and pull me over so they could see the engine in this little economy car.

On this particular night, I took my girlfriend Jean to Nashville. We were as deep downtown as you could get when I pushed on the clutch to change gears and the clutch peddle went to the floor and stayed there. I had no clutch and was in downtown Nashville on the first date with a beautiful chick. I had no choice but to keep moving. I told her to hold on as I put the car in first gear while the engine was turned off. I cranked the engine and both of our heads snatched backwards about three times before the Vega finally started. This got us going, but then the next light turned red. I now had to cut the car off and coast to a stop. Have you ever turned off a moving car? The backfire sounds like a shotgun. We would then sit at the congested intersection with a silent car waiting on the light to change. We were getting some strange stares.

When the light changed to green, we would repeat the process until we got to the next light and had to once again turn the ignition off. I learned that the car would actually start off in second gear which did not back up traffic as bad between lights. I repeated this one hundred and twenty seven times to get out of Nashville. We then headed south to The Z. We had traffic backed up at least a mile since I could only get the car into third gear which had a top end of forty miles per hour. When we would get to a straight stretch of highway, people would pass us and would give us sign language on the way by . . . even blue-haired old ladies did this.

We did make it back and as embarrassed as I was, it is now one of our most memorable moments. My wife tells our story best . . . about the southern Mississippi girl who had moved to Tennessee, got hooked up with a Mount Pleasant redneck, and started hanging out on The Z. Jeff Foxworthy would be proud.

THERE'S NO PLACE LIKE HOME

OOTERBILL, ALTHOUGH OLDER and grayer, still works at Victor and is still on perpetual probation. I still roll into town every year or so and will always make a couple of laps on The Z while there. Every now and then, I will run into someone I know, stop, and tell them some of these things I just told you . . . and many times I will learn something new about days gone by.

A new generation now travels The Z. Most of the former generation has long since quit traveling the route. They now hang out on the old wooden benches in front of Benderman's Hardware whittling and talking about the old days. I am sure that between these two generations separated by age, some of the stories are still passed on.

I am convinced, though, that many of the stories would be lost forever if not captured in these pages. The exploits of characters such as Tooterbill and Fatty Isabel would have slowly faded from the town's memory never to be known outside of the confines of Maury County. Heck, maybe some of the stories about the wacky things I have done rates up there with those guys. For the name Marshall McGaw to be in the same paragraph with them makes me proud.

Is there any other place like Mount Pleasant Tennessee? You now have enough information to answer this question, but I am going to let you be the judge of that. If you think there is another such place, you should write down what you know to insure the stories are preserved in history just as I have done. I do know that I have traveled all across this land and told these stories to hundreds of people and have never heard of or read about another place on earth like the place I still call home.

The End